T0077613

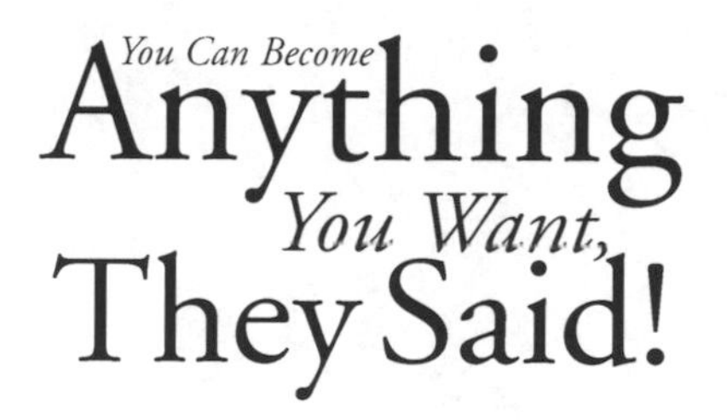
You Can Become
Anything
You Want,
They Said!

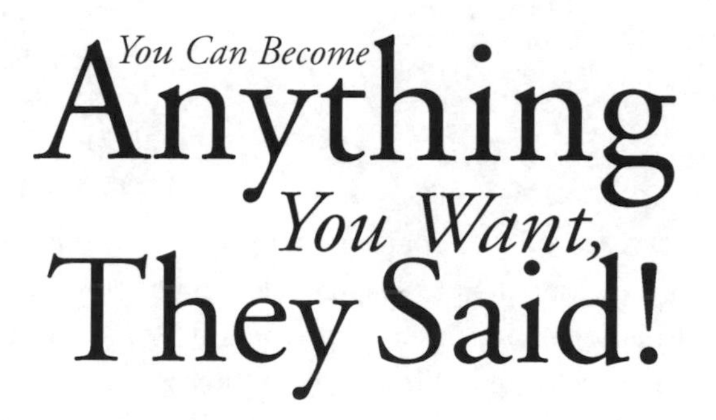

Anandini Valluri

ISBN: Softcover 978-1-4828-3726-1
eBook 978-1-4828-3725-4

To order additional copies of this book, contact
Partridge India
000 800 10062 62
orders.india@partridgepublishing.com

www.partridgepublishing.com/india

"What is joy without sorrow? What is success without failure? What is a win without a loss? What is health without illness? You have to experience each if you are to appreciate the other. There is always going to be suffering. It's how you look at your suffering, how you deal with it, that will define you."

These were the simplest, yet greatest words of Mark Twain that lived in my heart when I first read it and made me draw a parallelism with the life of a girl whom I came across leading a life which is quite different in this modern century.

It is a warm Sunday afternoon today, February 9th of 2014 sitting in my cabin beside the window and penning down a story for the first time ever since the release of my first book "Celebrating Life".

The success and confidence this book has given me is beyond words and I can only credit it to my dear readers. What took me three years of struggle to pen down every sprouting feeling in my book had got its highest appreciations in a matter of 3 hours. Those three hours may have looked glorious, defined me as a genius and many more heart filling words from my well wishers but the journey to bring it out and present it to all of you, always remains dearest to my heart.

I cannot just conclude it as my first book as an author but it was my voice, the anger and the years of humiliation that I went through in a world filled with "critics" and "confusions".

As I already said "When you want something really bad in your life the entire universe stands by you and it is for us to play the game and heart fully win every desires and dreams we have constructed over the years". Running on these lines here I am on this beautiful Sunday afternoon to pen down an experience with a very fascinating human being in whom I could relate my life's experiences and also discovered something new in me in this journey.

Dedication

If I were to dedicate this book to any one person, it would be an impossible task. As I wouldn't have penned down this massive piece if I hadn't reacted to the feelings of comparisons, marks and most importantly the feeling of "god dam exams" moreover if it wasn't for my neighboring aunties, relatives and the "the judgmental "attitude that has been deep rooted in our society, I don't think I would ever be able to find myself writing this piece of work.

Most importantly, I dedicate this book to the divine energy that was instilled in me to never lose my consistency and interest over this creative piece of work, if it wasn't for that I do not think I would ever discover a subject like this to ponder upon.

Though writing this piece of work had been a challenging journey emotionally and mentally, I wouldn't have been able to successfully complete it without two of my best friends support.

I am a very uncomfortable person to be with when it comes to facing my deep emotions and understanding relationship, yet if I were to conclude, I whole –heartedly dedicate this book to all the MOTHERS in the world, who are the most impossible subjects to pen down in words.

Acknowledgement

It would be incomplete if I hadn't acknowledged the support lent to me by my publishers and my agents for publishing my book and marketing it. Also constantly believing in my work and making my dreams come true most of the time. Their smoothness in work and management is admirable for a beginner like me.

Also, most importantly I have to whole heartedly acknowledge all my friends who readily agreed to be one of the characters in my book, considering their magnanimous outlook towards life, had inspired me to opt them as one of my most important characters to bring a meaning to the journey of my protagonist Vidhi. Sharma.

If it wasn't for you people and I do not think this story would every find a destination or a profound inner meaning to it.

Thank you once again, for always having the belief in me and never giving up on me.

Anandini. Valluri

(Author's Note)

This is not much of an author's note, what I have printed in this book is my take on what my protagonist goes through in a stereotyped and a chained form of education, that titles her to be a failure. The various people that have been in her life play the "game changers" to bring her out as the most influential writer's of today.

Contents

Chapter 1

This Morning

The event manager had called to check my availability for the sound testing and my requirements for the event.

Here I am in my apartment, a three bedroom pent house in the suburbs of New Zealand, a place that I fell in love with for its constant refueling scenic beauty. As I woke up to the bright sunshine and the overflowing positive energy within me, I could still feel my inner self dragging me on to my yoga mat for my meditation time in the morning. Though I could not manage to do it regularly I was able to successfully reach my target of doing it 5 days a week, being a 25year single woman, life seemed to go smoothly.

As I finished my morning rituals I head to my studio where I noticed my manager Edna had brilliantly placed my outfits for the event tomorrow. It was the release of something very dear to my heart in the "University Of Auckland". It was the most awaited moment and I felt a deep sense of responsibility towards this job, as I was being taken as a role model.

I decided to go to the venue. I sat in my car preparing my most awaited speech for tomorrow's ceremony. It was a long two hours drive along the countryside. As I sat in my car I was just thinking to myself on how creatively can I keep my speech small and interesting, most of all I wanted it to be an empowering event, as this was the release of a book on a very interesting person in my life.

As I was penning down it just made me smile to myself, the one word "Choice" a small word that had changed my life from becoming an engineer to more than what I prayed for.

The fact is "We plan and God laughs".

These were the pleasant thoughts running inside of me. Though my car stopped occasionally at one or two crowded places for signing a few autographs and greeting some of the people who adored me for my work and me as a person. I enjoyed this kind of love showered on to me on a regular basis.

I was living my "Dream of Happiness" at that very moment. These were the perks of me becoming a writer, though I don't stamp myself successful, as I feel there is more to these layers of life I have chosen.

There were lot of hands into the making of what I am living today but then my happiest realization was "When opportunity calls you to live an extraordinary life you have no right to decline it". It was a calling that changed the real person within me, who had excuses and regretted at the last hour of my day for having wasted my potential on nothing worthy.

It was a call to shut those cynics' mouths who echoed their hollow opinions.

That was that one day I can never forget, that helped me shatter my fears!

Today I feel it's a privilege to just sit back and rewind this one life changing story before I head to this event.

Chapter 2

The Beginnings

It was on the 4th of August at 7p.m when my grandmother and father were waiting for their first glance as the first baby of the house was going to arrive. It was filled with anticipation and the questions on whether it was a boy or a girl.

After a lot of rush and waiting for about 4 hours the doctor comes out with a huge grin over his face and says "Congratulations Mr. Vishwanath Sharma it is a girl".

Yes! That was my entry, I am Vidhi. Sharma and August 4th was my first day on this planet.

My entry on this planet was something special as I was the only girl in a family filled with an army of boys.

I was born at my maternal grandmother's house, a town near the coast of Andhra Pradesh, which had a lot of delightful experiences with truckloads of memories at the beach. Life was comparatively easy and felt like "living in the moment".

The luxury of eating in restaurants and best hotels may be one aspect of life but nothing beats the amazing summers on the terrace where the mangos were dried for making the staple and delicious Avakai (mango pickle) which was treasured for an entire year, in my perception I consider it to be a total art to make a pickle whose popularity never vanished. The best way to be eaten is by mixing the fresh made Avakai in hot boiled rice with a proper spoon full of ghee and mix it properly before eating, it's a dish only the people of Andhra can connect with. The craft of making it is very fascinating right from choosing the proper mangoes, the chilli powder, the quality of salt and oil, and every bit of it is a skill of its own, only grandmothers rule it.

This was a time where almost every kid in the house would participate in whatever the elders of the house did, unlike these days where kids are glued to their Xbox, PSP's, game boy's and internet. The fact is, by hanging out in the vicinity of the family's ongoing household chores, the kid tends to pick up the skills and also understand what his/her house does, which is how we learn our family traditions.

This was during 1992 to 1996, a time where the concept of internet, cell phones and computers were an absolute luxury. Honestly, I hadn't even seen them until I was 8yrs old.

I was brought up in an environment where my world revolved only around cartoon network, Mother's stories, homemade food, one 'Kwality wall's ice-cream' in a week and the general stores which was at the end of my street which felt like a huge shopping mall to me at that point of time.

My biggest entertainment was the never ending cartoon network, which started like a "suprabhatam" (Sanskrit word for morning prayer) with a huge glass of "complan" (chocolate milk, which I never drank fully!) the episodes of "Flintstones" with his caveman attire, his pet dinosaurs and his entire house made out of stones and the heroism of Popeye-"the sailor man" who always fought Bluto just with one can of spinach fascinated me to the extent that I imagined myself to be one of these characters. It was just amazing to see a hero in one's self in the fantasy world we live at times.

But then reality would hit me down when my mother dragged me to the shower to get ready to school. It was always a rush. Always! Starting with me forgetting my lunch box before saying a bye, to putting me in the bus on time was a maddening start of the day for my mother.

A time when I absolutely knew nothing about the world, no worries, no deadlines and no accomplishments. It was just blissful and artistic dreams and fascinations of every character that I came across, starting from my teachers, my family members to the cartoons I watched during this period.

I still remember a moment where I was so carried away by "Dexter's Laboratory" that I actually played in my back yard on a table with clay, mud, leaves and water assuming all these to be my potions and made all the utensils from my kitchen as my beakers and tools for my laboratory.

Well, coming back to the mad rush hour in the morning was always a crazy start for both my mother and me, as she was a working lady. What I hated the most was my lunch breaks, never did I finish eating an entire lunch on time in school, so half the lunch was brought home undisturbed.

I was a bright student in school but my mind was a can of thoughts and doubts which made me a very hyper active kid, who had many questions. But it was my teachers and my mother who would put up with me all the time and patiently give me a satisfying answer to everything I asked, literally everything. Though, I know the real answers today!

Travelling was a festival for me and my biggest journey that I ever travelled as a kid was the 2 hours journey to my maternal grandmother's place in a general compartment, it is not what it seems like today. These general compartments had a whole different world of their own the peanut sellers, the flower baskets in the trains, the tea and coffee vendors added a certain beauty to the entire journey. What's even more enjoyable is when you take a 6 am train there is a high possibility to sit beside the window and the train went through the fields and over the Krishna river, where we actually get to see farmers, fishermen, poultry workers and many other villages in this journey.

The train usually passed through the corn and maize fields, which looked like a brown and yellow carpet. It was always jam packed. But it majorly had government employees, bank employees and students who went to another town to study. What I can never forget is the fresh cut jasmine flowers being sold throughout the train and almost every woman in the train would purchase it.

It was a world of its own.

After this 2hrs journey, my heart waited to rush to my grandmother's house which was blissful and her welcome was always filled with mouth watering food and unimaginable pampering.

Though I love my maternal grandmother beyond anything or anybody, there were certain interesting customs to all the kids when they came home which was absolutely irritating at that point of time, but now when I think of it I totally get the science behind it.

It is none other than the "Famous group oil baths", to be specific I am talking about the time when I was 5 yrs old. It's basically an ayurvedic way of having healthy radiant skin, where we kids had to apply oil all over the body and then shower, so this basically removes all the tan and the germs.

What's very interesting was we were three kids, Karan being the eldest one among us always portrayed himself to be the well-behaved child, second was myself and third one was Mahesh, my uncle's son and we were the three musketeers of our time (the new entries were yet to come) and I was the only GIRL! And all three of us were made to have this sticky oil baths in just one go. This was one of the root causes for helping me have all the boyish fun I could possibly have as a kid.

A lot of the 90's born kids would know the fun of visiting railways stations in the night, I was one of them. My cousin brother Mahesh and myself where as Karan was always disciplined and soft spoken but his parents where the actual fun triggering people in our family, his dad and mom used to work in my maternal grandmother's town at that time and it was a festival for me to come over and meet my aunt and grandma at the same time.

In fact, I loved my aunt beyond anybody she was a very creative young woman and the brainy of our house. Her decisions had a sensible meaning and her say was final to every member, we were a unit and there was a certain bond among us where in we respectfully informed all our plans and decisions to my aunt as she was a pillar of moral support to us even today.

So coming back to the kids of this house, we were the brats of our house and we were very fascinated by the sound of the train and the different kinds of people we came across to the railway station. It's fun to stand on the platform and try to scream so that the trains whistle is in sync with our squeaky voices. What I can never forget is the time when Mahesh's dad (my uncle) used to take both of us at 7 pm to the railway station as there used to be a power cut in the entire town at that time for 2 hours and this is the only place which had bright lights all over the place. My aunt, Mahesh's dad and my mother were siblings so my uncle's house and aunt's house were no different from my own house.

So every evening all the kids used to meet up at my aunt's house as Karan used to be home from school by 3 and at 4 pm my mother or my uncle used to take Mahesh and me to my aunt's place.

That's where the fun actually started, as we three could meet up here and since my aunt was highly respected member of the house no one really worried about our safety or our discipline, but little did the elders of the house knew how much of a kid my aunt was, when she was around us! That's a secret only the kids in this house knew about.

So basically my cousin and I used to get into the trains as the railways station was right beside my aunt's house and it was a very small town and since they knew her well, we were allowed to enter the station without a platform ticket. It was an unfair exception only to us. So we were the only kids who got the luxury of entering into an empty train and just run around to our hearts content to the extent that we both ended up sleeping on my uncle's shoulder's on both the sides after all the fun we had in these empty trains and taken home, by then the power would be back and the rest of the family members could have their dinner peacefully.

The next day Mahesh and I would wake up confused all the time, wondering how we were at my aunt's house and not in grandma's house, by then my uncle (Mahesh's dad) would come to pick us. These were the most delightful forms of fun I would get to experience when I came over to my maternal grandmother's house.

I was a girl born in the coastal region. The waters of the sea was my hang out spot, the smell of the fish was what I grew up with and to be surrounded by cousins who were boys, had kind of made me tuff and fight at times as well, which proved helpful, though I am still a peace lover.

What I had exclusive among most of the kids during that time was, my dad who lived in a different country. Though I met him once a year, it never felt like I was away from him at all. I don't have an answer to that probably it is his gifts and toys that were always around me that made us feel inseparable.

There was this one time when my dad brought me a tent house, he had brought a range of stuff which many kids wouldn't have dreamt of at that point of time, starting from walkie talkie's, skating shoes, some of the rarest remote control cars, etc.

But for me nothing could beat the time I had with my cousins in my home town as we were not just blood relations, but we bonded tight. We considered ourselves to be "partners in crime" and "Best Friends Forever" (and we still are). One of the most memorable experiences was holding the coconut branches and swinging and having competitions among us to see who could hold on to it the longest. What we actually used to do was, in a backyard in one of our friends house which had only coconuts and mango trees, we kids went there every single day as this place was cool and we picked the mangoes fallen under the trees which made us feel like treasure hunters.

But then this place was never used by anyone, and so the entire place had branches growing aimlessly everywhere. Along with this we used to swing holding the coconut branches. It's beyond fun, just imagine swinging from trees with yourself high above the ground, it was for this particular moment that all the kids in the house waited for their holidays to come to grandma's house.

But then again all this fun was only at grandma's place, the moment we had to leave there was a sinking feeling inside me as I was the only kid among Mahesh and Karan to stay in a different city and met them once in every 2 months which felt like 2 years for me, the moment I got into the train a flash of the horrible lunch breaks with Mrs. Vaani Kishore watching me until I gulped my food, Mrs. Gayathri Prasad, my math teacher who expected me to solve the sums on the board in spite of knowing my stage fear and the whole concept of a "teacher" and the horrible school bus whose diesel smell made me hate my journey and worst of all, I was the last one to be dropped home in this bus, just ran through my mind all the time. It was hard to snub those feelings but it truly is a sinking feeling even today when I leave my grandma's house.

Silly they may sound, but these were my nerve wrecking problems at the age of 6 years.

Amidst all this havoc of issues I always enjoyed the occasional visits of my dad and showering me with chocolates, new frocks and dolls (I still wondered if he was a magician!!)

Until one fine morning…….

Chapter 3

The Best Gift Ever

In this ignorance and innocent lost world that I was in, there was no feeling of hatred or love or detachments. I see bliss in ignorance at times, but we are part of a social community and we are prone to be in the game how much ever we try to cut it.

I was absolutely consumed and confused in my lifestyle, as any six years old would have been. But never had it occurred to me that I never really had any friends in my neighborhood to play with nor was I showing any such interests. My world was my mother as dad was in a different country which I assumed it to be 4 hours away.

So basically, there was no sharing anything and everything by default was mine, worst of all anything mischievous happened was also my responsibility. This was an absolute setting which made me feel that the entire world lives this way, little did I know what was yet to come.

It just seemed so perfect that one fine day my mom told me that I am going to have a baby brother soon. Now, in India the gender of the baby is not told but it was my grandmother and my mother's strong belief and predictions that it was going to be a boy.

I still don't know what to expect or react like, I had no clue as to what she was saying but all I could notice was that my mother needed a lot of help and that the feeling of grandma and dad are not doing enough was what I felt. Honestly! I was being possessive about her and wanted to protect her more than what the family was doing.

So this was the first time at the age of 6 I felt the need to be a very responsible young girl, now this may sound a little over descriptive but the idea behind this is, a girl tends to feel responsible towards their family as the mothers influence is what comes into play. It's more like imitating in one way to be a grown up.

So coming back to it, I like any young girl wanted to be as much loving and protective like my father, so my biggest chores of the day would be setting all the toys back in the cupboard, putting my school shoes in the rack after I came home, not making mom walk around much by getting her water and medicines. Seriously, I was a disciplined kid once upon a time!

So now this was my new routine, I let some changes take place in my life by welcoming my new "Grown-up" self.

Until one fine morning everybody rushed to the hospital and later took me at 10 am. I was absolutely innocent and had no clue, nothing at all, I went in and saw a baby put on a table crying loudly, it was at its peaks of loudness. It really was. Initially I just looked away from the baby, as I was searching for my mother but an hour later I still don't know how all this happened but I was handed a tiny and the exact same baby whom I saw then, onto my lap.

Yes! That's right, it was the entry of baby brother Vaibhav. Sharma.

I saw a baby, a tiny human for the first time and that too on my lap, with a pink blanket wrapped around him, with hair soft like fur, with the tiniest of hands and lovely pink little fingers. The appearance was adorably cute, until it came to his crying sessions, which freaked the hell out of me!

The tone was a mid way between an ambulance siren and a fire alarm, which blew away my sleep for the next 1 year. Having a baby in a house is cute and adorable, but only when the baby is smiling and fed well, but the nights, I run short of words to explain the massive mess these tiny humans create.

His entry was rather unusual and unacceptable change in the beginning, but what worked well in my favor was my mom took me as a team player which made me feel my first ever and still my responsibility towards my little brother.

So now, this was the beginning of reconnection to my childhood seeing the way he was being brought up. He was my new little friend in my life for whom I waited for the bus to pick me as early as possible to just let me play with him. Every possible chance of bunking school was all that I looked for, to see him smiling and moving his little fingers.

Until he learnt to walk…

That's when the disaster began. Catching hold of all the wires in the house, running in the house, putting anything and everything in the mouth, messing up the place, jumping into anything they see.

They are no different from mini sized naughty panda's!

So there was this memorable incident, remember I told you about the tent my dad brought me. This tent was probably one of the rarest and colorful ones I have ever seen till date. It was a red, blue and yellow one in which 4 people can happily sleep. There was this one time where my mom planned a small picnic with me, Mahesh (my cousin), Karan(my aunt's son and the eldest kid of the gang) and their families to the beach. As our ancestral house was in a coastal region we were aware of all the beautiful locations in our place.

So this was my mom who is a very spunky and bright lady with some of the most unimaginable plans, out of nowhere she surprised us with this plan of taking my baby brother Vaibhav to the beach and our first family outing.

So, we all headed to pack our bags and all the ladies headed to the kitchen to make some pav bhajis, bhel puri and loads of homemade junk to munch upon at the beach.

After all the excitement of going to the beach with the entire family, my mother pulled out this tent from our bags to set it up. We were surprised to the extent that we began jumping and running in mad excitement.

It was one of the amazing mornings of my life. It was 6 in the morning when the sun was at the horizon, with the chirping sounds of the birds, a calm breeze, with the quiescence of the beautiful bay of Bengal which had bands of green, turquoise blue and this colorful tent on one side. What added flavor to this scene was the loads of fun with my dad coming to India for a long vacation, homemade food, all the kids singing and the waves of the sea breeze without any tourists, in the wet sand with our castles standing tall.

All the beauty on one side and here we had the little baby of our house who was taking his first tiny steps with my parents holding him in wet sand. My parents held is tiny pink fingers, as he was taking his baby steps in the wet sands, he was a very happy kid, smiling all the time as the waters hit his little toes. It was the perfect definition of adorable.

This remains so fresh in my mind that I could possibly never get that same clean and healthy environment I lived in at that moment, even if I travel another 20 countries. This was a greater part of my childhood at my grandmother's place, it was healthy with the family bond's, no responsibilities, just the innocence in our lost selves, having no reasons for laughing or screaming. It was pure bliss.

But every story has a twist in it, so did mine.

Nothing in life is permanent is what many say and so did I feel until this one day when …..

Chapter 4

The Shift

That's when my father finally shifted to India! I didn't know him or may be remember him much until he shifted to India when I was 6yrs old. I had no clue, it was always MOM,! Then MOM, BROTHER!! And now it was going to become DAD! Little did I know what was waiting!

His shift to India was a new beginning to all of us, as we were transferred to my first city experience, to the BIRYANI LAND. Yes! It is HYDERABAD.

Though I was told that I had been to Hyderabad a couple of times before this huge TRANFER! But to me this was my first major change that happened in my consciousness.

Life changed drastically, starting from a new house, new school and new neighborhood especially with a

Tamilian and a Punjabi family as neighbors. Everything was new and different but exciting.

It was my first time in a city at the age of 7 and complete new beginning. I was clearly waking up or growing up, so to say to the life I was being made to live, at that moment. My new school and new life was beyond my imaginations at that point of time. I was in my second grade when I joined this school and the first time ever that I made a friend here.

This girl was something interesting, she was alittle taller than me, with a neat hair cut, curly hair and always smiling, she was Naina. Until I met her I never had so much of an exposure to social protocols of being open and friendly to people, but right when I met Naina my whole life which was running around mom, dad, grandma and a new brother had changed or maybe it was put to a side for a while.

Naina and I were initially bus mates and all I knew or rather could notice about her was, she was hyper active like me and talkative (which was never "me" at that point of time) I am a Leo born in August, now it's a default setting for a Leo to crave for attention and that's exactly what wasn't happening to me, when Naina was around. I kind of started to feel jealous and lonely at the same time, but then again I never hated this girl at all. She had a certain charm to her that could not stop anyone from talking to her for hours together. She was absolutely bubbly. In fact at a point I started to admire her and wanted to be like her.

Though I was just a second grade kid coming to a whole new world and this shift was my first lessons towards reality and finding my true self. Though I never really got a chance to spend a lot of time with her, this was just like a spark that came and went away and remained as a memory.

And I was juggling with so many new feelings inside me, new friends and trying hard to fit in and at the same time I wanted to impress my class teachers.

I must say, I was a shy kid, really shy! I had nightmares of being called on and asked to do anything on the board. I don't know from where and why this phobia crept into me. In the beginning the thought of me being called on to the dais and being made to do something always petrified me until I actually and finally made the biggest fool of myself and the worst of performance on the stage one fine day.

I wasn't even having the words to explain my parents what happened in school. The fact is kids never say what they are going through as its hard for them to get the words out of their system, all they can express is the pain and irritation they go through which is nothing but throwing tantrums.

I totally and totally came in terms with those haunting nightmares and let it beat me up for once and for all on that one fine day. But then it was Naina, who of all the people appreciated me whole heartedly, though I clearly knew how much of a fool I made out of myself. This one gesture of her to encourage me no matter what, at a point when we were not completely "Best Friends" moved me a lot.

She was a different person altogether. That one little appreciation and push was a huge kick start for me.

That's the moment and the day I got over the phobia, the fact is human beings are actually funny creatures. Let me tell you, this one experience of "finally making a fool out of myself" had in return stopped me from having some of the craziest negative assumptions. Now that it was done what I was assuming until then, there was no space for another error to occur, never did I attend a speech unprepared and best of it made me highly spontaneous. I felt relieved and came out as the best speaker and still am.

This left an impression on the school staff, my first attempt at trying to impress my teachers. The real push behind it was the way Naina treated me as a person even though she had a huge set of her own friends and was always the bright student in school, she was basically a pure person. But this wasn't enough, academics where also a major share if you want to be an all rounder.

My mother used to sit with me every day and teach me everything taught in school, for a fact that she was a teacher too. She knew what and how I should be handled. If we trace back the idea to perform well, had begun in me with one new trait in me .... "COMPARISION". That's right! I was working on myself to be somebody and wanted the same glory and adoration and that's when I started to compare and compete.

This was an absolute healthy attempt as this helped me stay focused. It made me perform well, though Naina and myself were in different sections, we were good friends but not best friends by then but the school noticed us and gave equal importance.

Right when I felt that I was settling to this new change, here came the new twist.

Chapter 5

Another Transfer

Life was shaping up, I was getting myself accustomed to this new place and nerve wrecking neighbors.

By the way! I must tell you, believe it or not In India half the problems are born by our neighbors and my condition was no different. But to add to the mess it was a Punjabi vs. a Tamilian if this wasn't enough to add more to the mess all three families having kids of the same age in three different schools.

So that's the start of comparison, it does not just limit to marks, it starts from the school uniform to the architecture of the school building.

Remember my healthy competition with Naina that made me progress! But the situation at home was starting be quite the contrary.

What's interesting is no one speaks straight nor do they have the guts to directly mock a person, so they artistically sugar coat every dialogue which hits us like arrows. Though at that point of time it was my mom bearing these sugar coated arrows which constantly involved comparisons.

My Tamilian neighbor Mrs. Gajapati Pillai was a loud young woman who spent most of the time at my house. Unwelcomed! She had this peculiar art of verbally handcuffing people with the greatness of her kids, her work place and her renovated house and so on. You see! Every one is the heroes and heroines of their stories!

Though on the other side my Punjabi neighbor was a warm young lady who always sent one Punjabi dish every day. Mrs. Sahni and family were absolute foodies, everyday is a feast for them and since they came from a joint family their house was filled with guests almost throughout the year. So basically, it was Mrs. Sahni's food, Mrs. Gajapati's noisy entrance into my house, my school, my good friend Naina and a beginning of comparisons.

Life went on, Hyderabad was becoming friendlier and I was really in love with the city and my school but house was a mess, though it wasn't at saturations there was always a discussion at home regarding my school, my studies and everything.

Until one morning, on a warm Sunday, when mom and dad blasted the news that we were shifting again.

Right when I was creating a new world and trying to learn stuff like adjusting and settling to a new system. I got the shock of my life.

We were moving to Baroda, Gujarat. Now in the beginning as always I was absentminded totally when my mom told me this new place, in fact it took a little longer to even pronounce it, but then somewhere in my heart the flavor of new place and new life had caught my interest. I wanted to see it, the name was so fascinating that somewhere deep inside, maybe there is something I would get to see.

Every morning I went to school wondering how different would it be. But of all I was ready to shift as I wanted a change now from this little world where I wasn't fully comfortable but tried to be my best, because by now I was starting to face the pressure of my parents wanting me to do better.

I was a 9 yr old when I moved to Baroda, this was a whole new beginning from the basics. Life here was around a proper "Gujju community". What I truly love about it and still can't forget was, these people are passionate businessmen, they are very humble, family relations are priority in their households and what's even beautiful is their colorful Bandhani saris and amazing dhokla's. It's very basic but a whole new experience for the baggage that I came with from a town near the coastal area to Hyderabad and now Gujarat. My school was also multi cultural it was my first time I met Parsis, Jains, Christians and best of all the school celebrated each of these festivals.

It was an absolute new place and a new start no annoying neighbors and no comparisons. I was just myself and bonded with my new classmates and Mrs. Karuna my class teacher.

There was once this memorable experience for which I never thought my parents would allow me for.

I had my first learning's on what independence and being away from parents felt like, at this one point of my time.

It was a camp in the forests of Gujarat, firstly it was a shock to see an offer to go with my friends to a camp which had a safari, trekking and two night stays at an age of 9 yrs, secondly my parents instantly agreed, without giving it a thought at all.

This camp taught me my actual basic survival skills, as this was far away in the outskirts of Baroda, and our accommodations were in a tent with 9 others sharing in the middle of two huge banyan trees. It was absolutely the most beautiful trip I have ever been to till date. The mornings were bright with a huge field of Daffodils and the deer swiftly running near the pond in the forest. We were sleeping under the stars, around the camp fire, there was loads of Maggie, soup and some bread being cooked for dinner. We were kids and yet there was a new sense of bonding, attachment.

Though I was close to Naina, my best friend back in Hyderabad this was a new opening on how to socialize apart from discussing marks and the next teacher coming to class or competing in class. It was a joy and a sense of calmness within me. I started to love this place, I was having the time of my life, watching the peacocks dance to the rain, the various creatures and the waterfalls made me wonder how beautiful our country is and how little we know about it.

The scenic beauty of the morning sun over the hills and the chirping sound of the birds with a cold breeze and fetching water from the windmills erected in the forest was the actual life I witnessed in my 3 days stay.

These three days had an impact to the extent that I can picture the scenes and those moments every time I close my eyes.

But then again, it was a matter of exactly six months that I started to see a change in the house. My parents had heated discussions, they were absolutely uncontrollable and I was always clueless. I was back home from this trip and nothing new happened apart from going to school, studying, playing with my brother. Though I was finding it monotonous my parents started packing the stuff in the house again. It was strange in the beginning, we had just come to Baroda and it was only 7 months but here we are packing all over again.

It was the first lesson of my life that I was meant to be a traveler and home is where we four of us stayed together. Though it was an early shift for me, I had to get used to the fact that we were shifting because of my dad's job.

The fact is every time I see huge cardboard boxes I get those butterflies in my tummy, a new place and a new school all over again.

Until one fine day, I realized that this discussion was about me and again my studies but this time, it was not a comparison but the biggest question again, if I could stand.

A NEW TRANFER!

Chapter 6

The journey

My parents were highly concerned about my studies, my well being and my adjustment to a new place all over again, as it was third school a new city. They were being sorry for me, but some things were undeniable. As this was about my dad's career, though mom was a school teacher she took a break as my brother was a baby. And this time it was a huge start for all of us as my dad used to work in the "Holiday Industry".

I haven't told you much about him, but the fact is to him it was his bread, butter and heart. To me this hotel industry job was in a way an exposure to the different shades of the glamour world as it was filled with staff parties, loads of guests from different nations, celebrities. Though it was a secondary luxury we had a glimpse of the real picture that goes in the making.

It's a high end stressful job, the business is all about people. As here it is the question of whether you're a F And B manager in a hotel, or a kitchen porter working behind the scenes or if you're involved in the management of a hospitality business, every time you come into work your making someone's day that little bit better. Thanks to my dad for actually opening up and showing us the world and the different types in it.

He is a man who thoroughly enjoyed dressing up in suits, various ties and always maintained a polished and yet a charming appearance. It was not just his appearance that was crisp but his attitude and thinking which was deep to the extent that none would imagine the capacity of his decision making powers. He carried himself with a certain sense of style and piousness within himself that caught everyone's attention. He was indeed a very charming person. This was the kind of man I lived with in my house.

Whereas my mother is one of the most out spoken persons any one would come across. She is a feminist in her thinking, she had the capabilities to push her boundaries to saturation levels and it's not an easy task at all. She was extremely ambitious and thirsty to learn and implement new things be it in her work or home.

There is a certain sense of bravery element in my mother, which I could possibly never find it in me at any point. You see, it's not possible to inherit everything. I call her brave for the fact that she solely managed the house for 7 years when my father was working in a different country when I was a baby, during a time when Skype or at least a cell phone was not accessible. I call it the "landline days". Honestly, in today's situations relationships are blossomed through phones, which is in a way ridiculous when compared to my parent's time.

These were the kind of personalities I was being brought up with, so the fact that we moved to new places every now and then was inevitable considering their career choices, we kids got accustomed to this as this was my family's reality.

So this time the tradition of mom coming over and telling me happened little differently.

My brother also joined this discussion! Yes we were kids, but we were made to sit and told that we were moving to Pune, Maharashtra.

I still remember my mom showing me Pune in a map. It wasn't a shock to me anymore, by now I know the pattern of adjusting to new school, new culture, and new life as these were my share of the problems in my version. I was ready as always. My mother feels she is lucky to have a cooperative daughter!

I was making up my mind, as I learnt to self-soothe myself from the hurtful feelings of detachments we develop when we leave our best friends, cousins and the place we love. But then finally we came down to Pune as per the plan.

It was all over again, cleaning, packing, duct tapes and thermacole all over the house. After all this packing we finally landed in Pune. It was during the winters when I first reached there. It was a freezing 3 Kms drive from the railway station to our house (we were provided by the company). It was a different start altogether.

It was a colony we stayed in and for the first time I started to play with friends in a garden there. Though I socialized with everyone I still had issues getting along with the needed amount of flow. I always had a mini gang of my own and this time it was Tina A.K.A Manisha, Amrutha and Rhea. These were the three girls I started to hang out with. I am a girl who came from a really different background and I needed to be molded.

These were the three girls who majorly, unknowingly changed my total perception on making friends and openly speaking. This was the beginning of "speaking my mind". I literally hanged out with them every single day. Honestly these girls actually taught me cycling, proper English and a total different approach on grabbing opportunities.

As days passed by I started to come to the ground alone and ride my cycle for hours and hours until one day I spotted this new girl in our colony whom I had never met before, I was curious and at the same time something was holding me back but then I don't know what made me talk to her, I instantly went up to her and introduced myself.

This was my first step in curbing my fears and stepping up, I was feeling good. After some random chat I understood that she was Paulomi Pal from Calcutta, who was exactly like me when I shifted the first time, it was so strange to meet a person who had the similar mindset and fears, we were hardly 10 yr olds and surprisingly we were from the same school. I noticed this when I got into the school bus! Those days were different but silently I was going through the process of a personality development.

As I understood at a very early age that networking with people is the only way to understand a new city and a new life. Moreover, it does not help if we try to shy away from socializing as, somewhere at some point the people we meet end up as the biggest lessons in life.

That city was magical. Comparitively quieter than most metros but not enough for the big city experience, Pune is an eclectic mix of cosmopolitan culture and contemporary thinking, strung together with a strong sense of identity and tradition. Anyone and everyone can easily fall in love with the life and the climate of Pune. The schools and colleges were not factories that manufactured graduates but actually produced some real quality people.

Within 10 days of shifting my dad put me in a Christian missionary school for the first time ever, I was in an ICSE board school and it was at this point of time the doors of me started to open up.

All this while, I was being a good student and disciplined but that wasn't enough to sustain a competition as it was my school that made me realize my very first lesson on how important the attitude and our personality is than just numbers.

Every kid was special in his/her own way, everyone had an individual identity to talk about, what made them exclusive among ten others is what my school had fed me with, in my 2yr journey in Pune.

What's peculiar is, it was my class teacher Mrs. Alifiya who believed in me, this was a real push, for the first time I was getting attention and I was being noticed for something apart from just books and marks. I don't know what she believed in me or saw in me but there was always a certain spark in her eyes when I went up to her and put forth my way of doing any work I was given.

The morning school assembly was a total make over as this was my real exposure to actually connect myself to some spiritual power. Oh by the way! I was just 10 years old at this point of time and I know the word 'Spiritual' being used at that point of time may sound a little big, but the truth is, every assembly in school we were made to sing the hymns and read the bible every single day. I don't know if God exists or not, nor do I call myself an atheist but I could feel some strength in me every day. I never really gave this a deep thought but I didn't know what was waiting.

This was basically my life in Pune, but it was not exactly as happy it may sound. I was coming out of my cocoon and starting to build myself.

Everything was settling up but I was finding it tough to put up with the ongoing discovery of the self to the competition of being "Exclusive". My maximum potential was tested, but was not even close to satisfactory. My school was too demanding, this one way was helpful as it made me work beyond my imagination. But the sad part was I couldn't explain my parents what exactly life was, the pressures of being better than the best and the expectations and priorities your very own classmate would get in front of you just by a very simple reason most of the time, I found it frustrating what it was like at school so eventually it only made them feel that their daughter was performing poor which was linked again to the sugar coated arrows and the comparisons, making my mom feel all those fears to be true.

Things weren't going perfectly well, my marks were deteriorating but I was given as much of an importance as a topper was given. It was turning worst to the extent where my mom felt may be I was 'Off the track'.

You see this is a typical mind set! Marks are student's horoscopes, no matter how good, famous and extraordinary you are outside, your intelligence is somehow DIRECTLY connected to these numbers. However extreme we are at a certain activity, the depression of "not doing well in studies" never leaves our parents.

Let me explain how this madness goes about in our country. The only possible root cause is the attitude and the fear of failing is why passions are not given respect, where it needs to be nurtured. What can we say? It's not the parent's fault too! It's the race for acquiring the basic necessities in a luxurious way, so you think parents would let you do anything else? I can't generalize this but if the attitude is different in terms of welcoming failure and accepting it not by the kid but by parents the whole perception would have been different.

The fact is India celebrates mediocrity of their neighbors and definitely the victim is the kid. Now think to yourself, why there are so many youth suicides and depressions, well! Coming back, I was seeing the beginning of hell, as school was too demanding in terms of marks and the work, I was trying to live the facts and expectations of my parents, without giving a thought on what exactly I wanted for myself. Amidst all this once again we had to shift for the fourth time, do I really have a choice now? Not yet and never again as I clearly had no control over situations.

and this time it was..........

Chapter 7

Back to Hyderabad

Yes back to Hyderabad! My first love!

I was glad and this felt like a breath of fresh air as the change was coming at the right moment. As always I was ready to shift or may be more than ready this time.

If you noticed the pattern so far, the moment I was happy and getting along, settling down a storm of changes were happening to me.

It was piling up inside me, every time new place, new school, new friends, it would be unfair to say that I hadn't enjoyed or explored around.

This time I was finally back to Hyderabad. Guess who my neighbors were!

Mrs. Sahni and the very famous, Mrs. Lakshmi Gajapathi Pillai. No kidding!

I couldn't remember all this back then as I was a little girl(I later learnt this was her nickname but, that's a different story). I felt this was my final and last shifting. In one way, I was happy as I was going to join the same school in which my best friend Naina and I studied earlier.

So on one fine day I went back to my school. Well, this was technically the first day of my school and I wasn't feeling home at all, as the infrastructure had changed completely. Everything looked smaller to me, including the school, play ground and the swimming pool. After seeing around, it was the time for my morning assembly, I recollected the quality I saw back in Pune, where morning assembly was like a visit to a temple as all the teachers and students are expected to participate in the liturgical observances and prayer services that form the rhythm of school.

This includes Morning Prayer in the chapel, prayers at Morning Assembly, prayers before and after meals, prayers before competitions and examinations, Prayer Services and celebrations that form part of the observance of the Inaugural Assembly, and here, I am in a typical "School", where everyone is fidgeting in the line, seeing the sky, one is setting his school belt, their hair or the tie. I was new to this class, absolutely I knew no one this time, though I studied in this place once, yet I went and assembled in the class line.

It was an absolute shock when suddenly to my left, a girl with short curly hair, with two of her front teeth resembling more like a rabbit's teeth and little chubby rushed and stood in the line.

I don't know what happened that very moment but then she suddenly took a glance at me, I was a tiny girl with long hair, petite personality and thin. She just burst out from nowhere, so stunned and frozen to see that it was me ....Vidhi!

After a little while of seeing each other, and questioning nearly ten times in our heads.

It finally struck me that it was Naina standing beside me and this was the actual unforgettable moment when I felt I was home. I was meeting her after three long years, it was so beautiful. Until then all the complaints I had in my head just vanished after meeting her.

I was paraded the next one hour along with Naina to the staff room and the friends in the other classes. She was excited and glad to see me, though our friendship was brief it felt like a warm welcome to me.

It was beyond my happiness. It was such a miraculous moment to have met her after a gap of 3 yrs and yet she remembered me as a good friend. I was touched. That was so "Naina" a person of values and deep respect for friendships.

That was my very day of school where I felt important and not judged just invited warmly and I was in the happiest space that one moment.

What's interesting is, if you remember I was a bit jealous of Naina when I first met her but the dynamics of my relation with people were totally different this time.

Naina and I were now best of friends. I was a totally a new person. The fact is back in the Christian missionary school I was taught the art of "being prepared". I was shaped in terms of my personality, attitude, my character and my approach to academics though I wasn't able to give it my 100 percent I was a struggler back then.

It was a whole new chance given to me to prove that "marks horoscope" is still glittery. I was performing well, this time. The expectations from the school weren't exhausting and best of all I had friends who became a family. Though there were moments when I missed those times of bible reading and the hymns. It was definitely instilled in me, the curiosity to know my real self.

It was my very first beginning of deep thinking process. It was a silent curiosity to find and hear the clash of the inner voices on a certain decision.

But these thoughts never stayed for long but when they did they never left me.

Well, this was my take on life at that point of time. I was now in Hyderabad, re united with Naina and a whole new personality. Started a new life with a bunch of new friends specially Varsha, Komal, Ankush, Dheep. It was a lot of fun teasing, playing together, and jumping around from bench to bench. What still remains a memory to me was the time when we used to tease Ankush. This guy is something totally out of the box and I would need another book to write about him. The whole idea of teasing him was to provoke him and he was beyond smartness all he did was smiled and gave us ten more reasons to tease him. He was just an amazing friend. Every day was like a fairy tale and everything was collective fun, right from writing our class tests to having lunch!

I was finally able to get along with the people in this new school easily. Some people have been along through this journey so patiently, in thick and thin when I think of it, it's nice to sit and chat all those moments over a cup of coffee today.

Though my house was a mess, the great Mrs. Gajapati was uncontrollable, comparisons were a part of my daily meal! She was right across the hall, almost able to hear even the sneeze that came from my house. Seriously! Neighbors can go to any extents.

I digested it and walked away all the time, as I was the kind of person who could not voice out spontaneously. But the rage, the anger and the hatred which were in the sapling stage were growing within me.

But what always kept me calm was the fact that I had a school and a bunch of friends who showered love, wanted me around, felt good in my company and found me humorous too. This acceptance was an entire world to me and this was the only reason that made me wake up to all the alarms in the house and rush to school. Honestly, I waited for the next day to come.

We were together all the time right from the school bus, we shared, laughed and had done tons of pranks. I felt alive every second when I was around Naina, Ankush, Dheep and Komal.

Everything was good and peaceful …! Nothing seemed to be an issue at that time. I was able to make peace with myself, right until another disastrous news broke out.

No not a new transfer! But this time it was a new school in the same city. What was happening behind my back, what was shocking and what was unexpected all of a sudden was the major reason behind the life I had to “break free” to choose.

Chapter 8

It all started here

I was absolutely devastated, I broke down completely. I was furious as to where did this thought of putting me in a new school creep in! What are they even thinking! Do they realize how much it took me to settle down with all this love and friends! Do my parents even understand and see me what I am going through! Those were my unanswered questions.

All I knew was Mrs. Gajapati felt this new school that came up in a better locality had quality and she being my "well wisher" and brain washed my mother.

The fact is, when your child is compared not directly but in a way that makes you as a mother feel "may be my daughter is not in the race" "she needs quality like the neighboring kids" "what am I doing as a mother!" these are the basic thoughts that pester parents when a third person enters the already existing tensions in a family.

And it is their utmost care and fear that their daughter is being left behind, where as the daughter may have the life which is beyond any treasure in the place she is in and the world she has created for herself but the feelings don't reach out each other. That's when the child silently suffers, throws tantrums, performs worst than before and that's when you lose out the equation as a parent and a child.

This is the general scenario that happens at least in one of three houses. This is the basic reason or may be the start of children drifting apart from parents emotionally, they may appear happy and joyous but that's just a façade or the inability of the child to express his/her feelings considering the possible reactions.

This is a very simple logic and this was my exact condition I was going through my entire life, here I am happy in my space and building my peace and out of the blue I am put in a school all of a sudden and the culprit happens to be a neighbor. It was not easy dealing with a non stable life at the age of 12 with no stable friends around all the time. The thought of a new school and a new place always drained my energies out, as I had to start everything from the scratch.

I find it insane even today!

I was tired and exhausted with these thoughts, I felt like I took more than what I could bear at that point of time and nothing really was under my control, it was an absolutely helpless situation. It was silly to first consider some neighbors words so seriously, second of all who was she to enter into my peaceful life?

I was in a rage or anger but all I could do is cry to myself in my sleep every single day. Every single day, I cried to myself saying everything will be fine, people will love you and tomorrow will be a bright day.

These are simple proverbs but I was actually telling them to myself before sleeping to come in terms with something I wasn't ready for at all nor prepared at all. I don't think I was even given a choice, it was just declared and that was final.

I woke up the next morning, hopelessly gave an awkward smile to everyone in the house and calmly put on my uniform and got into the auto I was arranged to go from now on. My first step in to the auto broke me into pieces inside thinking of the moments with Naina and me in the bus, I never went to school without her, with Mrs. Banerjee our sports teacher and a very lively young woman in the bus with a few other students singing songs along and talking everything, every possible thing in the bus just rushed through me. I was helpless, broken and left with no choice but to calmly go into the auto, where 7 of us were sandwiched and dropped in school. Initially, I had a lot of thoughts running as to how this new school would be or how would I get along with people all over again. One of the most haunting thoughts was would I rebuild the same happiness I had in my previous schools.

I was new to this school, well practically the school building was new and no one knew each other at all. At the first look of it, I hated every bit and inch of the building. It was just one huge evil building looking into my face, with huge glass windows and one hoarding of the previously passed out tenth grade students and their marks advertised, possibly on every wall of the building, which they believed themselves to be "trend setters". Honestly I didn't spot much of a difference between the hoarding which showed a 50% discount on clothes and this one over the school building.

As I walked I was anyways feeling hopeless and not really anticipating for anything new or awkward as I now understood that this school was not something I would like in any manner even if I tried to.

Until the moment I stepped in and faced the shock of my life. MY SCHOOL DIDN'T HAVE A PLAY GROUND!

"How on earth can a school not have a playground!" was my instant thought, I wanted to cry my heart out. It was unacceptable and impossible to imagine to live a life like that.

I was already exhausted by then due to lack of sufficient sleep. It was impossible to sleep ever since I was told that I would be in a new school.

And seeing this disaster, the passage like classrooms made me have enough. After venturing around the place I was finally taken to the class where I was supposed to go. I was a 12 yr old practically the first days of entering adolescence and the most insanely awkward time of any one's life.

So here I am in a new classroom. I hated every inch of it and I was disappointed to be a part of this mess. I missed my old school, my time in Pune and Baroda, were all flowing as memories in front of me. I know I wanted to cry out badly, but I had no time or space for listening to my inner feelings. But I knew clearly I had to live with it for a long time.

I didn't speak to anyone around me but I used to just blindly listen to everything in class, take notes as this time I was not in a school but it was a factory. I call it a factory for some valid reasons first of all this school didn't have a play ground, so technically it was no play but only work, secondly it was just one huge building on a main road and thirdly, it was all about grinding our day to day chapters in class and just stamping the same during the exam time.

This was the "school" suggested and expensively advertised by my beloved, most caring and highly "well wishing" neighbor, the great Mrs. Gajapati pillai.

This lady has done it, she finally started to rule over the minds and manipulate. Foolish people were the ones who were manipulated.

So here I am in an unimaginable mess and an impossible situations, to my parents these issues didn't bother as long as the "numbers" were there on my exam sheets at that point of time. I don't wish to portray them as feeling less but it was the society that was structured in such a way that parents are also trapped in this mess. Though they knew it was ridiculous, they simply had no choice but give their daughter away to these "systems".

I was still the same calm, lost person in the corner of the second bench and I haven't spoken a word with anyone except to those teachers who asked me to introduce myself. It would be a shock all the time when I compared my real self to the past days and the time I had moved to this new abandoned zone. I knew it in my head that I had faded out from the real bubbly self that I was, I knew I was faking every bit of smiles I flashed at people in the house and at my school.

Until one fine day three late admissions joined my school, they were two girls and a guy.

As I never spoke to any one I never really sat with anyone in a bench I preferred sitting alone, as I wanted to be cut from people. I was mentally locked up in my head but these girls just came and sat beside as this was the only vacant seat beside me and this new guy sat in the row which was beside me. It was a gap of half an arm distance. I never spoke much, I was still the same silent and calm person just copying notes and my class teacher happened to notice this about me.

So in order to somehow make me more lively and interactive she made me the class monitor, I was initially a little reluctant but then I had no choice and one fine morning after sitting with these new people for about 3 days the guy beside me opened up.

He was the cutest guy I ever saw, hazel brown eyes, light brown hair and fair. Strange it may sound for a hyper depressed person like me to notice an adorable looking person beside me. The fact it is, it looked very obvious he was a very charming person. This is Aarav.

The first time I saw him I couldn't even pronounce his name, I wasn't interested in talking to him as such as I was still dealing with my issues of changing into a new school unprepared.

This new guy Aarav was totally different, all I could remember was he would do possibly anything from screaming in the middle of a class to probably throwing pieces of chalk pieces at you, just for attention. And this time it was for my attention. I never understood what he was up to all the time. First of all he was so amazingly cute and second of all he just wanted to irritate me and somehow make me talk.

It was clueless and this went on for two months, to the extent that he started to tease me, stand beside me in the assembly line, make his friends talk to me or send messages through his friends.

And worst of all was following me in and around the classroom. He was doing all this just to bring out the maximum amount of talking I could possibly do. It was irritating initially, but then I could see the sweetness and come back to myself in this process, I needed to "live in the moment" and I could see it by now I had changed a lot I used to wait, every passing day to see what this guy would be up to, I was fascinated for the fact that he patiently took his "precious time" just to somehow make me talk.

I know I was being ridiculous but I was just not interested in anything, the anger in me on Mrs. Gajapati Pillai just lived there in the corner of my brain, heart or possibly throughout my body, but I couldn't let it go nor forget about it. Though I never bragged about it near anyone.

After a certain point I finally broke this mad silence which I was building and trying myself to be isolated. I finally started talking to Aarav. Sometimes it's important to reciprocate the same energies and time which people invest in you, just for your happiness.

I started to talk to him I wanted to know him and why was he doing these stuff, and the only logical reason was he just wanted to prank me and talk to me to see my reactions and expressions. It sounded very different to me for the first time, I was puzzled. He happened to be the most generous and selfless person, I ever came across. In fact, it still surprises me.

It was now the beginning of finally opening up with the other girls in the class, in fact what's surprising was I was a topper in class and it was my first time or may be last too! Being a topper in class was a perk but the ego of Mrs. gajapati's point in me joining the school in one way had won. Which made my parents even more drawn towards her "wise words". It was simple luck, which made Mrs. Gajapati aunty look like the angel in the story, if I hadn't made it through, I would have probably enjoyed the role of a "victim" in my story. Well, destiny has its own plans.

So there was a certain amount of attention the class gave me as I was a topper and I was treated as this "brainy kid". But the fact is it was simply a factory, where you just grind with or without understanding and empty it on paper.

Which they hadn't noticed it. So somehow I had almost the entire class starting to talk to me, borrowing my notes and they wanted to know about me. After a whole research on my entire life they finally got the history of me coming from Pune to Hyderabad, from a really good school and now transported to this new "factory".

It was shaping up all over again, these people in this school would talk to you only if you had marks and if you were this "brainy kid" I know how insane it sounds, but a lot of parents out there don't know or understand that a kid, their own kid is judged and made to feel inferior about a "number" that is the root cause to hit an entire personality growth of the child. But this is the fact!

I was feeling a sense of anger and confusion about the education system in our country and was in search of answers.

Anyways, it was one side of me doing the self-search while I was in this "new factory" or school, trying hard to make peace with the life here.

I was having a certain level of respect in this school just for these "numbers" and on the other hand I met this guy Aarav who was completely opposite to me, he was crazy, mad, noisy and spunky. All he would do is plot plans to make me talk to him or get a huge bunch of people from random classes and have fun. Academics was not his thing!

What's surprising was I was starting to like this new person, in whom I was able to see the fun person I once used to be, but couldn't connect much.

Day's started to go by, I was liking this school, though it was filled with numerous flaws, I was tasting the flavor of being a topper in school for the first time and also a new set of people who looked up to me in this process.

The fact is I was entering my teens and this is the most crucial and awkward phase of any person's life as everyone turns to "grooming " and tend to become obsessive and I was no different from this, I was getting my share of attention in terms of looks and brains. So it felt like an entire package!

So back to school!

Aarav was the new best friend whom I waited to see and wonder for all his master plans and acts he would pull out every single day.

I was starting to like him, having him around filled the day, and also became my reason to wake up every single day.

I liked his personality and by now we started to talk, it took me about 3 months to finally go along with the flow.

I started to enjoy my conversations with him as my class teacher made me sit beside him, with the hope that he would write his class notes at least by seeing my notes!

Makes me laugh when I think about it now, as I was turning out to be more like him. I learnt to enjoy life in a simple manner and wherever I was. What's interesting is, at a time when people were collapsing seeing their "marks", parents coming to the parent-teacher meeting and expressing their sorrow's about their child's performance, here I was with this guy who totally gave no importance or worried regarding any of these "mind wrecking" issue's. He was the most relaxed and happiest person any one would come across. I really didn't know much about him but I know his personality, which never gave me a chance to even ask him where exactly was he is from or where's his house or whatever, though by now we were pretty close.

It was a very new beginning and I was totally in love with this school, never gave a thought of the times with Naina, Ankush, Komal and Dheep or the time in Pune and those mesmerizing morning assemblies or the time I went camping in the forests of Baroda. All those memories remained as my treasured experiences and kept aside in my heart. It was a collection on various aspects of growing up, that added layers to my personality, in many ways it was because the various people I came across who shaped me.

This was the extent of happiness I saw with Aarav in my life at that point of time. Yes we were kids, but beyond that we were best friends and interestingly Aarav had no bit of a clue of my past. He was more of a "today person"!

Everything was settling down once again and life was shaping, hopes were high and there was peace within me when I was at school, but my house was a living mess.

I absolutely hated it……

The anger never vanished, it was there right inside of me, the desire to just break out and say "I know what I want for myself" but it never had the right fuel inside of me to bring it out. I needed more concrete reasons to voice out.

Chapter 9

The IIT bug

My house had a complete opposite life to what I was going through in school, Vaibhav (my younger brother) was a 6 yr old now, he was in his pre-school and still the adorable baby of our house, my dad had completely shifted to India and my mom was working as a science lecturer. I was a 13 year old now and life was a bit comfortable.

But then, it was during this time when I first heard the word "IIT".

Now in south India just like the festivals Pongal, Ugadi and Onam, getting an IIT seat is celebrated with the same zest and importance. If getting an IIT seat was considered to be "godly" then engineering seat was supposed to be a "tradition" to any south Indian family.

And if you, thought my house was quite opposite considering the different places we moved to, you are totally wrong! As my house was also following these traditions.

What's really funny when I think of it is, Mrs. Gajapathi, my annoying neighbor started her endorsements on IIT coaching in my house, she started off again with the victory stories of her daughter bagging a seat in an IIT coaching center for which there was another separate coaching to get into the actual "IIT coaching center". RIDICULOUS!

It was absolutely ridiculous and made no sense at all, if the formula to crack a seat were these coaching centers then every south Indian should be an IITian.

But coming back to Mrs. Gajapathi, she was the "support for her future IITian daughter" I remember her daughter as this machine, who woke up at 4 in the morning with a chemistry text book in hand and a glass of milk in the other, she was in this position until the school bus came, the rest of domestic chores of getting ready to school, having breakfast, etc was done by Mr. and Mrs. Pillai while their daughter was holding the book in her hand.

I always wondered if she would just blast out at one point.

This girl was probably the only girl in the entire apartment who was hated the most not because of her, but her mother. The fact is she had this weird routine of waking up at 4 in the morning at the age of 12 and coming back from school at 4 and going for an IIT coaching center till 9 and again studying till 12. I don't think even farmers made their cattle work this much! (just saying!)

If this routine wasn't enough Mrs. Pillai barged into my house every now and then explaining the wonders of this "disciplined coaching". My parents were a little interested but then I was clearly and absolutely not interested nor did I even show any interest as I had my own life going well in my school.

It was not a surprise for me to see my parents initially showing interest, as it was Mrs. Gajapati pillai's decision that they fell into and put me in a school which was more like a factory. Though I made peace with it, with my own self-support and people like Aarav, just made my day making me feel loved and appreciated. I did have the memories of my past to hold on to whenever I felt exhausted with the people I had in my life. It was like a "switch-on" and "switch-off" mode for me. I always missed Naina, Ankush, Komal and my spiritual connection with the energy and the mornings in Pune.

Seeing my neighbor's daughter, my mother felt why not her daughter also give a try, but she failed at putting me in a coaching center, there was a lot of regret in her for not able to put me in the same grilling sessions and "qualitative education".

It was nice of my mother to have huge dreams. Dreams, which I could possibly never dream of, which were glorious to fantasize but the truth is they were being dreamt by her and not me.

This is a typical issue in almost every house hold, everyone dreams, everyone is born free and individualistic in their own opinions, but it is the love of parents which appears so harsh for us to achieve as we are constantly trying out ways to keep them happy. But the fact is if it was us painting our own dreams and achieving it there is no chance of regret on both the sides.

This was exactly lacking in my house, here I was a girl who had a baggage of changing nearly 5 schools by now, and shifted to 4 different cities in a span of one year, hopelessly throwing myself into every new situation that came by, making a life out of unimaginable circumstances, trying to get over the pain of missing the people who loved me and still letting the neighbors and family decide or do anything they want!

I was highly and strictly against this coaching, I had ENOUGH! I was tired inside, there was piled up anger and sorrow that wanted to tear and come out. But all that came out was tears of helplessness, unable to voice out what I wanted as I dint know what I was searching for. Is it love, success, freedom?

It was a phase or beginning of confusions, but the only thing that kept me happy and cut myself away from this inner voice noising around in my head was my time with Aarav. I was constantly able to feel the vibes of regret at home, for not putting me in a coaching centre which I was bluntly against.

Even though I had Aarav and loved to be with him around, deep down inside me it was just an 'escape mechanism' to be away from the house.

Somewhere inside I was waiting to leaving Hyderabad and again move away to some far off place. This was to this extent that I went through just because of a neighbor and her opinion, I can't blame her a bit. The fact is people only discuss their opinions and feelings it is for us to be stable to hear it as a third person talking and leaving it there, but some of us take it till our bedrooms, kitchens and everywhere.

This is exactly what I went through at that point of time. The only person who could hear my pain as a kid was my aunt (my mother's sister) she would actually argue with my mother on how senseless coaching a person without even knowing what it means is like, I absolutely loved her for that. She was my voice and stood by me to support, why would anyone not like being supported!

My mom hadn't come in terms with it, though she mellowed down a bit on that subject. She was an ambitious woman who wanted to give the best of things to her kids, but I on the other hand wasn't able to receive it with the same positivity.

In this chaotic environment after a lot of discussions and arguments, finally I came to the conclusion that I wasn't going to bother anything that was going around me. Literally anything. I was slowly locking myself up.

Chapter 10

Travelling was my savior

My life was a living mess, when I was at home. I had nothing directly attacking me but it was the silence, the failure of parents not in a position to convince me anymore, the fear inside me of "not being up to the expectations". These were basically self created worries in me which is nothing but stress. I was suffocated by living up to people's expectations and all I had to do was, work as per their reactions and hopes, it was pressurizing inside but I didn't have the voice to bring that out, at that point of time.

This is an issue faced not just by me but my surroundings were filled with people who were going through the same phase, I sometimes wish there was brochure on life.

All I wanted was to cut myself away from these social norms, people are very sweet, so sweet that they want to bring a revolution in their neighbors house, when their own house is on fire. But the protocols say "behave well and respect ". Seriously! You think so!

But the only peaceful part of my life was spending time with Aarav I hardly knew him apart from his name, but that was my only 'calm zone' and a point where I felt like a happy kid.

Under all these situations, my dad declared another transfer.

Was I happy? No …!

I WAS OVER-JOYED!

This is exactly what I wanted, I just wanted to go out of these protocols and attacks of neighbors with their loud advertisements on "IIT".

For the first time in my life I was thrilled to go to a new place as I always wanted to go to a far off land and this time it was "Africa". Yes! this time it was Africa, to be specific it was an Island country called "Seychelles" spanning an archipelago in the Indian Ocean. It is to the northeast to the island of Madagascar.

Though there was sinking feeling, I was sure inside that I was not able to take the environment around me. That's the way it's been with me throughout my journey, either I am trying to adjust at times, either I am happy with someone or I am put in a new place, nothing in my life seemed permanent at all.

I started to believe that nothing really stays with me for long for the number of times I drifted apart from what I used to settle down for. I was a traveler and I had to learn to live with it initially but now it was my life. I started to like this travelling. It always introduced me to new shades of my very own self. I was travelling within myself, as all these people and places gave me different perspectives.

But this time it was different, we were shifting to Africa to an Island called "Praslin" in Seychelles.

None, of our family members had heard of this place, it was completely new to all of us, but my dad, an adventurous man as always, decided to go with the entire family this time.

Vaibhav was a 7 yr old now he was also a part of the transfers and adjusting mechanism.

It was going to be a huge shift from what I was going through.

It was at this time when we started to Google about this new place and possibly get to know all the details regarding "Praslin. "Praslin" is one of the archipelago islands of "Seychelles", it's a dream location for possibly anybody on this planet. What's interesting is when you look down from the flight you will find that the islands are like a Chocolate box, placed on a blue satin blanket.

Trust me, people talk about dream destinations and destination weddings or beach side weddings, this is the exact place where one should be, I can safely say that all the best beaches of India on one side and Seychelles as a whole is beyond imaginations and on the other side, totally! It's filled with valleys and trekking, camps, forest visits and Bungee jumping were the first learning's of my life at "Seychelles". If this wasn't enough Cruise lines and beautiful crafted Victorian house boats were my hangouts in this place. Prior to settlement of the islands by the French in the mid-18th century, Praslin's Côte d›Or was a favourite haunt of pirates.

The island was named Praslin after the Duc de Praslin, the French minister of marine.

This is where the legendary Coco-de-Mer, the world's heaviest nut, grows high on ancient palms in a primeval forest. The Vallée is host to six species of palm to be found only in Seychelles.

Praslin stands at the forefront of Seychelles' tourism industry. It also provides a base for excursions to neighbouring islands, which are important sanctuaries nurturing rare species of endemic flora and fauna.

What I learnt about this place is they do not have the concept of agriculture whatever they ate was basically imported from Australia, Kenya and India. They spoke French and life here was not "like a fairytale" but "was a fairytale".

This was the kind of place I was being transferred to, technically my dad.

We, specially my mom was speechless, she had tears of joy and unbelievable to see her that way. It's a very rare sight you get to see your mother so happy, I could see her appreciating possibly every bit of the surprise my dad was showing us.

It was beauty everywhere and this was our first time in a flight and to a place which hardly people knew about.

What else could I ask for!

I absolutely wanted to be cut away from my old life, I needed an escape plan, I tried my level best to make peace with my surroundings, I failed dramatically, I was unable to even voice out what I felt.

THIS IS EXACTLY THE KIND OF PEACE I WANTED!

I felt it was the right time to move out of the mess I was going through at Hyderabad, but what could I possibly do. If destiny could bring me to Seychelles, I believed that it would re- unite me with the people I cared for. Simple logic, which I threw myself into.

I was in a land where every fraction of a second I could feel the word "peace", what else could I possibly wish for.

At times I felt if it really was happening to me or was I just in a dream. It was hard for all of us to leave India, specially my parents and their parents but it was needed. If you want something, something real bad, you got to let go a few things. I wanted to instill, peace in me, though I was an absolute kid, I just wanted to be away from people at that point of time.

And here I was in Seychelles, my day usually started at 6.30 am and we stayed in a cottage near the foot hill, and this was the first time I wanted to see an adventurous new self in me, this was basically born in me, seeing the regular citizens who lived there it was a huge island and the population was 60,000.

Life here was not so "Indian routine" of waking up early, rushing in the morning to leave to school or anything, nothing remotely close to what I was during my stay at Hyderabad, Gujarat or Pune.

Seychelles was a life where I woke up at 5 am to the sound of the rain drops trickling over the leaves, my cottage was in the centre of nearly 7 almond trees, it was a huge cottage with a veranda, a huge garden in the front yard and the backyard, we had coconut trees, curry leaf plants, banana shrubs and drumstick leaves in the back yard. It was huge and all this right under the foothill. So, every morning was not bright but a sense of peace and lush green trees and leaves everywhere, welcomed my morning. Since we lived in an island that did not support agriculture, there was no concept of a vegetable market in "Praslin". My brother Vaibhav and myself, did not have any friends at that moment and we did not join our schools yet, so technically we were doing "home schooling". But there was this one day, we were so bored and exhausted with the never ending beauty of this place, we were cut from the Indian channels completely. The only time we felt that we were a part of the real world was the time when "BBC channel came in the morning for about 4 hours. The rest of the time it was just French and Creole (the local language).

This was the condition at home, and we had no clue what we could possibly do to entertain ourselves. So, this one morning Vaibhav came up with a creepy idea, by now he was a little boy, who was exploring the world around him. He made a plan to see what's it like to climb the hill that was beside our house.

It was a very bright idea as we were tired of practically doing nothing. From a time where I was constantly compared with the neighbors kids, neighbors intruding into my house, trying to bring a revolution in my life, this new change has finally brought me to a total new life of isolation from real world, though it was amazing it was boring too.

Since Vaibhav came up with such a great idea, I was just ready to go and I was always curious to know and see what exactly is there in that hill which I could see every time but never thought of going into it.

Finally, after convincing my mom, the journey began. My brother and I took long sticks for support as we started to climb, we had a bottle of water, a scarf (just in case) and one umbrella.

The starting was a steep slope, which was initially exhausting for us to climb, as we were kids. Vaibhav and I held hands as we were slowly climbing with our long bamboo sticks that we had plucked from our backyard. This slope dehydrated us completely and finally we got on to the first level of the hill.

To our wildest imaginations, we saw an orchard full of oranges, proper fresh oranges to the left side of where we were standing, there were nearly 50 trees which grew aimlessly. We were so taken aback and what came after that was beyond description.

We saw a Mango orchard to the right, this may appear unbelievable but trust me, these places exist and they are safe. All you need to do is pack a bag and aimlessly walk along any road that came by your way.

And we kids were doing exactly the same. This mango orchard was such a beautiful sight, that I get goose bumps as I am describing it. It was a yellow and green carpet of mangoes everywhere. It was an aimless journey, no hopes, no expectations and no pre-conceived notions about the orchard, it was such a simple journey, that brought us to an unbelievable surprise.

It had bunches of mangoes almost to every branch of the tree. There were hundreds of oranges and mangoes just lying around the trees and interestingly it's not a land owned by the government or landlords or any one's property, this was just wild vegetation that kept happening from the birth of these islands and no one really wanted to disturb its natural growth.

What's interesting was, we kids were not scared or felt lonely in spite of being on a hill without anyone around us, we were with each other and all we were aware was, just one straight road if we had to go home, so as such there was nothing to worry.

This sight of oranges and mangoes were so tempting that Vaibhav and I collected whatever we could in our hands and bags. We were so thrilled by the view of it that we couldn't stop ourselves from walking further.

It was a walk of another few steps that we saw a randomly thrown layer of sweet potatoes growing there and carrots. It was the first time in my entire life I was plucking a vegetable out, a properly grown and healthy vegetable out, all by myself, we were absolutely overjoyed. Most of all, we were dying to see our parents reactions to what we have discovered in this land.

We started to pluck and store in the potatoes and carrots in our bags, this did not end here. As we walked further, we noticed chilly plants and best of all, was the huge tree whose leaves are famously used in Biryani's and lots of Gravies. It's the "Bay leaf". A lot of us don't know that the tree of a "Bay leaf" produces cloves and its bark is the "Cinnamon".

These were the stuff we picked up in our "adventurous trip". I personally started to bond with my brother from this point of time, it was here where I actually slept on that messy grass, without fear of any insects or anybody to come and disturb in those vegetations that we were in, I was at peace with the world and myself. I was able to hear my own breath and the sky was so clear, that I never saw a blue color of that sort to this day.

It was bliss, it was heaven and this is what my destiny brought me to after the humiliations and the comparisons back home.

After a while we realized it was time to leave as mom would be worried.

To the shock of her life…..

Chapter 11

Parents joining the fun!

She was absolutely speechless to see her kids in something she would have never imagined. We put down all the fruits and the vegetables that we collected on that hill, on our dining table. It practically covered up the entire table, more than surprised my mom wasn't sure as to what to do with so many stuff. She was totally unaware of what this place was until we went and did this famous act.

The next day my parents were curious to know and see its beauty as Vaibhav and I went on describing the beauty of the place the whole day, which couldn't help but to go and see as to what we were talking.

In fact we described it so much that my dad had to take a leave, just to explore what we kids saw.

As planned all four of us decided to go again to the same place, so we started off early in the morning. To my surprise my dad was so impressed to see this hill and the beauty of it was so mesmerizing that he was in a state of shock.

Life is so busy. We are no different from machines living with machines in our house and at work. Do we ever take time out at least an hour a day to be in the lap of Mother Nature! The fact is "we are busy being busy "as one of favorite author said!

It is impossible in a world filled with concrete parks and ridiculously huge buildings.

This was a proper and most needed vacation for all four of us.

My brother, though he was a 7 yr old and I was 13 were lucky in a way to be in a land which was just so full of trees, berries, fruits and vegetables. All growing wildly without any chemicals or any sort of research being done over them.

My family was at peace with themselves. The whole "IIT bug phase" was slowly fading.

It was here that I was calm within myself and lay down to recollect my baggage full of memories with my cousins at the beach, the time we had our family picnic at the beach, the tent house, the Christian missionary school, having a small brother, new friends, new people everywhere I met and Aarav. I was possibly living all my moments as I lay on the partially wet ground under a mango tree. I sure did have an amazing journey so far. An incredibly gifted journey.

And it came to this point at this hill, which finally made me open up, my mother and I started to come in terms with each other, I spoke my heart out on what

I was going through personally though she tried to understand, we didn't really connect much but we did come to a certain level of peace.

Though she excused me from taking "coachings" but she never gave up on building that "fighter's spirit" in me.

But the topic of engineering was still a mess. We had the arguments and coldness over the subject. Like any mother, all she wanted to see was her kids to be successful and also become definitions of success.

But the fact is parents hardly notice the fact that, kids struggle, go insane and fight all the time just to see that 5 mins of happiness on their parents faces, just for that few minutes they throw possibly all the tantrums and everything.

It was clear that my mom and I were not in a position to give each other what we wanted. We were coming in terms with each other on this subject. The only reason we were able to have a calm and peace talks was the background that we were in. The place instilled peace, insanity though I was tired inside myself, Seychelles was letting me relax for a bit.

We were so much in love with this island that the next day my dad decided to go into the valley's present in this island.

As per plan we got a huge pick up van and all four of us drove to the end of the island to visit a valley called "le valley de-mai" it's a French name. Vallee de Mai is a valley in the heart of Praslin National Park, an area which was untouched until the late 1930's and still retains primeval palm forest in a near-natural state. This palm forest includes the endemic species coca de mer, of understanding universal value as the bearer of the largest nut in the world. There has also been a body of legend which has developed around them.

What's interesting about this valley is it had no wildlife at all, but was filled and covered with humongous trees whose fruits were the size of a jack fruit called "coco-de- mer". Its Seychelles primary and important fruit. It is used during feasts, celebrations and carnivals. More like representing the "spirit of Seychelles". It was a huge one, probably double the size of a jack fruit with a very shiny wooden crust like thing. This was roasted with some coconut and the shell of the fruit is broken and eaten. It has a jelly like sweet substance inside the fruit and the outer wooden layer is used as a bowl. So this valley happened to be the home of this fruit, and it's Seychelles, the only country where it grew in.

We started our journey into the valley. It was a deep, dense forest with the rarest form of peace I ever encountered. The most beautiful part of this journey was we could hear the leaves falling from the trees, so that was the extent of calmness present in this part of the world.

I was absolutely living every step I took in this valley, spotting possibly some of the rarest varieties of birds. What's interesting is that at a certain point my brother, Vaibhav and I spotted a green lizard, its body was pattern green. It was so beautifully camouflaged with the leaves that we couldn't notice that it was a lizard until it opened its eyes. It was just remarkable to see a creature like that.

Vaibhav, was a kid but he was experiencing some of the rarest things around him, not even aware that this is nowhere close to what we live in India.

And here I am a girl who by now had changed so many schools, places and people. Seychelles was a huge break from the past.

It was a beginning to re-connect with my inner voices, life was shaping up in Seychelles it was calm and had given me ample time to think to myself. Though I had a chance to think peacefully as to what I really want to do with my life and what I was really looking for, I wasn't sure on what I wanted to be. I wasn't ambition less but I was confused as to what is this whole existence all about, what am I doing "here". These were my thoughts on a daily basis. I woke up to these doubts which had no words to put them out. It was intense at times, but I pushed the thoughts away by involving myself in other activities. I was young to subject myself to the understanding of soul searching but silently without understanding or awareness I was undergoing the process.

There were times when I felt if it was only me or my brother, Vaibhav who was confused and lost as I believed that the whole world is like me and thinks like me. Innocent it may sound but that was a fact within me.

Chapter 12

What was I Searching for?

In my beginnings of 'what is going around me', inside me and what I am subjecting myself into, life was not simple. I had materialistically everything I wanted in front of me, which any normal kid of my age is never provided with, yet felt like a helpless person from the inside. These thoughts piled up within me due to the massive comparisons I saw during my stay in Hyderabad. When a person is compared constantly the question of what he or she is stems within, to find what is it that "I am" made to be.

Confusion is the beginning of thinking. Restlessness is the search for answers to your confusion. Frustration is the beginning of implementation of the rough plan that undergoes massive editing in the mind.

Seychelles opened my doors of confusions, until one day when my parents gave me the same periodic shock of my life again, they decided to shift to another place.

Well, by now it was my seventh time and it was in my DNA to adjust, explore and understand the whole life from the scratch in a new place and a new neighborhood. So these was nothing to think about or collapse over as now I was meant to live it this way. A new country and a new city, which is completely opposite, is what was waiting for me this time!

It was Saudi Arabia…

Yes, after changing 7 different places and getting along with possibly everything emotionally (with the neighbors in Hyderabad) and physically (to all the hills and valleys of Seychelles) my dad decided to move to this new country. SAUDI ARABIA …!

I was totally and totally done with travelling, was what I thought when I landed in Seychelles after travelling via Maldives and Mauritius which made me and family visit and go around sightseeing. But never did I imagine I would go to the Gulf region.

Remember, in the beginning I mentioned the fact that I was the only girl in my school whose dad stayed in a different country, Well! It was Saudi Arabia, and here we are heading back to the place where it all started. These were the words of my mother.

I could feel the same sinking feeling that I had when I was leaving Aarav, Naina, Ankush and Komal. I came in terms with the fact that nothing is really permanent and so was with my shifting to new places. It was absolutely a challenge all the time to start everything from the scratch. But the perks of this whole process is

I got a chance to see new people, new cultures and new perspectives that I could take along with me every time I left a certain place.

Seychelles was a definition of heaven it was hard but then again it was not my motherland to be my permanent house address. I had to leave Seychelles I had no choice.

Finally after all our exit documents were ready the packing began in the house. It was one of those many dejavous moments of huge cartons, tape and scissors all over the drawing room. Packing all the clothes, the books and the crockery items carefully sorting them into different huge boxes to send them in the cargo.

Vaibhav and I were kids, but we were sensing our feelings, we clearly did not want to leave a place like this. A place where we practically plucked and ate anything and everything without re-thinking anything, walked along the streets, beside the beach, playing in the backyard, our occasional visits to the hill top, the trekking, the valleys. It was hard emotionally to disconnect from all this and completely switch on to something so contrastingly different.

So, as I said the whole packing was done and it was just 2 more days left for us to leave. I don't know what propelled me but for one last time or may be the beginning I just wanted to see the beach where I spent most of my day and the hills and those orange orchards where I walked in. It was quiescence everywhere. Practically everywhere.

I was connected with the Mother Nature, I could feel myself in her lap laying down in peace, just with me and my inner most self. I had tears trickling down to the thought of saying a final goodbye. It was hard, really hard being a 13yr old not able to understand what I want, what I am looking for and what is the meaning of my existence. I was calmly laying down deep in my thoughts, just feeling the massive calmness and the breeze.

I lay down on the soft sands of 'Anse Lazio beach in Praslin(the island I stayed in), with my eyes closed feeling possibly every ray of sun touching my skin and thinking to myself about my whole life was filled with travelling, each time each place gave me a solution to deal with smallest of the common issues everyone had but, the places the ambiance I lived in all the time gave me answers to many issues, at a time when I was just seeing world. Right from the time I was with my cousins at my grandmothers place, I learnt the actual meaning of bonding, my family and how to sustain relationships with everyone being an active participant in each other's life, my first stay in Hyderabad when I met Naina and the personality makeover I had, to Baroda which shaped fears into bravery the trekking and forest stay was my basic lessons to survival strategy, my stay in Pune Christain Missionary school had instilled a sense of spirituality, taught me the importance of morning prayer, which built in me the ability to question myself, made me see the world around me through my inner self, it rose massive doubts on my existence, which eventually my journey took me back to Hyderabad where I was subjected to real situations with worst of comparisons with no answers, making me a hunter for answers to why and what is all this about, to add more to my journey it became more extravagant by shifting to Seychelles, a place, that finally made me hear my inner questions, though I still couldn't find the answers to what I was doing in this world, why was I running on the script written by parents or my neighbors or the society, I just found one clarity by coming to Seychelles.

Initially I couldn't understand what I was thinking or even notice that I was having massive confusions to understand this whole concept of existence and doing what others tell you as a sign of respect, but now it was the calmness that Seychelles brought in me which made me realize my questions, it made me hear my own confusions raised by my inner self, I was able to see myself as a third person and hear my own queries, though I still remained without answers. I knew my questions well!

Every lesson I learnt was by the people I was meeting and the cultures that had a strong influence on my ideology. The tension that lived between my mom and I calmed down due to the calmness I was witnessing at Seychelles, the adverse effects of neighbors invasion into my family's decisions were all coming onto a platform and an understanding. In a way we were coming in terms with our stupidity around us and how we were victims of these situations.

After an hour of this time travel I left the beach and was set to leave Seychelles.

New hopes, new questions and new lessons coming my way.

I don't know what I wanted but I sure realized that I have to search my answers of this inner voice making me run from place to place.

However weird it sounded, that was my real self and it was the beginning of my definition to the self.

My questions were simple I wanted to know how I evolved, what is this whole thing about God, is it just a powerful energy, why am I even praying, what was it I am existing for and why I am I constantly trying to fit into a “neighbor’s lifestyle”.

Chapter 13

Take it as it comes!

I was a 14yr old and I had these kinds of questions in my mind, where girls of my age had major concerns on pimples, new outfits, crush's and thoughts on dieting.

Strange it felt, I tried being the girly person I was witnessing around but it was a major lesson which said "everything has an expiry date, including the façade we put up, it's like walking in scorching summers with make-up on, you may protect it to a certain point, but it's got to melt when you reach your final destination'.

So this one thought had changed me as a person in every possible manner, I was thrown into some of the most unbelievable places anyone would see and here I am again going on a completely new adventure and new learning's. After all the packing, the emotional good bye to our neighbors and our one last walk in the garden we were finally in our flight to India, it was a calm 6 hours flight happily went away in sleeping to some of my favorite French and Creole music of Seychelles.

I finally woke up to the landing call and fastened my seat belt and my spirits were high as I was jumping in excitement to meet my grandmother, my aunt, my uncles and my most favorite cousins Karan and Mahesh.

I imagined that scene of receiving them in the airport like a Karan Johar movie, a zillion times. It was a great landing and finally touched my mother land and my first love, Hyderabad.

The city had the same charm and beauty, there is something about the city that I can never put in words, may be the happy mornings or the fun life or may be the culture, I really don't know what it is..! But Hyderabad always catches my interest and never lets me leave a second without enjoying.

Even in my worst times of comparisons with Mrs. Gajapathi Pillai's daughter Hyderabad as a city never let me down.

After a gap of one and half year, seeing my folks at the airport was bliss, tears of joy, hugs and loads of family gossips went on throughout the night.

The best part was the feast and the amazing food my aunt and grandmother prepared for us, this is what family means. Nothing changed, not even a bit the never ending love and the warmth I received from these ladies of my house was something, eternal.

This was just a mini vacation for us, as we had come for our visa stamping by the Indian embassy to leave to Saudi Arabia.

Whatever may be the time period I was given, I just wanted to make sure I had the best of time I can ever have that I have missed over this gap of one and half year with my cousins.

The entire week went in shopping, going around the city, checking out new shopping malls and catching up all the movies that I had missed out.

It was a crazy week, since Vaibhav was an 8 yr old; he was a part of our gang too.

Though he was a new member in our team, he was family, so the blood was equally contaminated with the "Sharma family's" craziness as we were a pack of hooligans.

Though the questions and the spiritual aspects travelled everywhere along with me, I was never really a religious person, I went with the flow of things. It was a family week for me.

Until the last day,

We had to leave to Saudi Arabia, if I remember it was a flight on a Monday as usual the entire family, send off, hugs, kisses and tears were flowing all over the place. It was a complete dejavous moment for me.

This time I was being totally mellowed down, as I wasn't excited as much I was for going to Seychelles.

After all the sentimental scenes and everything I was at my gate with my boarding pass, totally lost in thoughts and the mad fun I had over the week, I was missing all of it. But then I found this brochure on Saudi Arabia which was beside my seat, which kind off fascinated me.

I started to flip through the pages to see what is this place all about? Do I really fit in? How do people even live in deserts like this?

To my biggest surprises ever, the moment I started to read this book I was deeply and very deeply lost in to it, so deep that it was impossible to stop imagining what this experience was going to be like.

I was kind of taken back to the beginning thoughts of "why the hell am I even travelling again", just an hour ago to "I badly want to travel". All thanks to this one brochure which was left by some passenger, which made me curious.

I did not want to stop reading, I took it along with me into the flight as my parents were busy setting the cabin baggage's and settling down, Vaibhav and I were on our massive expedition into this book.

Little did I know an hour passed, that the flight had taken off and we were well fed by our host on Emirates, but what came after a gap of three hours was remarkable.

I WAS 42,000 FEET ABOVE THE DESERTS OF SAUDI ARABIA!

Now that's what created butterflies in me. I was thrilled to see a land completely filled with sand, just heaps and heaps of sand and camels walking around over the place, this was a total phase shift from the take off to Seychelles and the remarkable beauty of the Indian Ocean 38,000 feet above sea level.

Seriously! How could I not enjoy something like this? I couldn't wait any longer to get down and see this beautiful place.

I was reflecting upon my thoughts again, how silly of me not dreaming all this that I was witnessing around me just a few hours ago!

I wasn't welcoming enough for these creative images in my imagination as I was so lost in the luxuries of being loved and pampered by my family members in India.

But it sure had more to it. The beauty of a new place, specially a desert filled with red sands everywhere, sand dunes, camels and what not!

I was finally in the city of gold - Dammam (a city in Saudi Arabia). Life was settling now, new school, new beginnings and new people everywhere. Time passed by and now I was in my tenth grade.

Despite aspiring to be a modern state in many respects, the Saudi nation still has one of the most traditional societies worldwide.

I was witnessing a change in me, I was open, I was more calmer, I had a certain definition to me, I was turning out to best at my communications and I now know the right amount of diplomacy I need to put in. I was able explore my mind in areas of spirituality and happiness, here at Saudi Arabia.

Tenth standard it was and the most crucial time for parents as I was going to face my board exams, though I stayed in Saudi Arabia we still followed the Indian CBSE syllabus, I can't say I was an obedient student but there was something in me which was calling me all the time. It was a desire to live independently and see the world, Saudi was a big change in my life, the culture and the lifestyle tempted me to see what other countries looked like. The whole journey, my school and my people were such an integral part of me that I was finally a girl who was starting see my questions as my dreams.

I knew somewhere deep down that I was searching for answers on what I am, who I am and what I am doing in this world. I was now seeing these questions as my inner most dreams to run after, but I was still a part of this social community I can't run away without living it.

Tenth grade turned out to be one of my achievement years, I was happy with my score and now my mother felt I was having the engineers quality in me.

I know from nowhere I am talking about engineering!! well, here's the thing she had this strong feel in her that I am extraordinary, though I never felt it myself, she had that conviction within herself that I was beyond my own imaginations of myself. I would say it's a mother's love that radiated her energy on me and so engineering was her choice for me.

With this dream of her's to make me an engineer though she exempted me from IIT after massive heated discussions I decided to leave Saudi Arabia.

To begin a new life in India alone, without my parents and my brother, Vaibhav. I don't know if it was the right choice or not, I didn't even know what I want, but all I was dealing within me was the question of what I really was up to.

I was feeling hopeless inside myself. I did not know what I wanted. All these years I was going around places seeing new stuff, experiencing new stuff, I thought I was having the most of freedom, but I was trapped within me and myself in my quest for what exactly I want.

It was clueless inside, my inner voice gave me confusions but never decisions. I was being ruled by this voice, a confusion that woke in me lived its luxury inside me as a confusion always but if I had ruled myself

I would have had the power to make it into a decision. This was my first feeling on what it feels like to regret.

I decided to come to India finally.

But what I sailed through this, is nowhere close to imaginations.

Chapter 14

I needed to know

Saudi Arabia, a land of camels, I have always been a "beach Person" but this was a new opening.

I landed at the King Fahad International airport, right from the moment I stepped into the airport it just blew my mind off.

Where do I start describing this from! it was a huge or may be let's say a gigantic airport, with some of the best sculptures of the various Arabic personalities, this land has a huge history.

In terms of religion, culture, trade and civilization and what's interesting is though it was very tightly bounded to the values, the customs and traditions, it had its own style, Arabs are famous for their lustrous lifestyles.

This was my first exposure to what it takes to be your very ownself, grounded, rooted and yet impactful.

So, here I was lost in seeing this amazing airport and people walk in long white robes, with a head gear and a red checked cloth beautifully draped on the heads. And women, in unimaginably beautiful long black robes with scarfs ranging from basic to designer wears.

It was strange to see all this for a girl like me who lived a life in Seychelles, where all I could see is very casual dressing, in slippers and hats to something so contrasting with people in clean crisp outfits, make-up which was so edgy and yet traditional.

What's interesting to watch all through my way to my house in Dammam, was that this was a stylish city, it had a mix of brands from the west and also the proper authentic Arabic merchandise.

It's so astonishing to see this, deep rooted culture, specially for the fact that in Seychelles, though it was an African nation it was more of French.

But Saudi Arabia was one land, which was never invaded it has never lost its identity and this was really beautiful to watch.

I was in my car, sitting by the window, just watching everything around me which absolutely appeared like postcards.

To my left I was so amazed to Luis Vuitton stores, Armani, David off, Gucci and Dolce Gabbana, some of the most high edge fashion stores in the world and to my right I see Starbucks, Dunkin Doughnuts, KFC (the original one), Burger King. I was more like "is this a movie or what"!. I was speechless, what can I even say or even dream of, that too coming from a place where I was surrounded, or should I say more like lived in trees, bushes, orchards and waters of the beach. This was the beginning and opening to what world looks like, how different cultures live together.

We drove by all the noted stores of today, some of the most authentic interior designer stores, French fashion and some of the high society restaurants of all times.

Everything I saw here in the beginning was like a DSLR picture. It was materialistic but yet had a certain sense of beauty to it.

This is and was, SAUDI ARABIA!

To this day I have no clue what it was written in my destiny, it was me who had a random decision taken in my mind that out of all the luxuries I was living in.

After I moved to Saudi Arabia I somehow got the chance to see Dubai, Bahrain, Sharjah, most of the gulf. Well, also it was a habit for me to journal down all the experiences I went through when I visited these places with all the pictures, and descriptions and feelings poured into it. And my journal was pretty huge by that time it had a lot of leaves of memories buried inside from the time I left India to Seychelles, Mauritius, and Maldives to Possibly most of the gulf countries.

It always reminded me of who I am and how routed I wish to be to myself. I could not afford to betray my inner voice, this time as well it was this inner confusion that made me do something unbelievably wacky!

I had explosive amounts of peace and happiness, I lived inside a seven star hotel practically every single day for almost 5 years of my life, a centralized ac atmosphere, with world's edgy fashion streets, with some of the best quality food ever, it was always a dreamy style of living. Not an affordable one if my family ever decided to have it privately in Hyderabad.

These luxuries were totally because of my dad and his career growth.

Though I was very happy, I wasn't remotely connected to reality. Everything I saw or felt always seemed like a dream, I tried real hard to convince myself but I knew it wasn't happening at all. I was sinking day by day into materialistic happiness.

Though the city looked so colorful it had the highest amount of Muslims living here, of different nationalities.

I never knew Islam was born here, considering the fact Saudi Arabia was the country which has Makkah and Madina, the two holy places for Muslims.

I was absolutely stunned at the devotion and richness of religious traditions that the people followed here.

They wore their cultural attire, though they lived the best of life they were still some of the most humble religious people who prayed five times, with a sense of devotion.

I may understand or not what prayers meant but it was just impossible to imagine as to how a person can be devoted and actually stay connected with the highest self within him.

This was exactly what I was looking for, was what I felt.

Seychelles was my land of questions, India was my land to "live in the moment" but Saudi was the beginning of witnessing my answers.

I needed a direction, I needed to know what was I upto in my life, I wanted to connected with myself. I knew how hopelessly I nodded my head to my parents wishes, friends wishes and neighbors wishes but this time I needed to know what I wish to do.

My mother always told me, I am a free person.

But I never really connected to that statement anytime, it was a process, Saudi was starting to sink into me and now Saudi Arabia is my new favorite address.

It was beyond happiness or maybe I wanted this kind of a lifestyle all my life and started to realize it.

It was a huge change from what I saw in Seychelles. Though I felt more real in Seychelles, Saudi was giving me the chance to detach a bit from regular realities of work, competitions, life and everything. It was different one moment I am in some of the longest and largest shopping malls and the next moment I am understanding my lessons on devotions and prayers seeing the massive number of People praying all at once, properly five times a day.

What I imagined to be an impossibility all throughout, proved me wrong and showed me that there is one part in the world where people live to the fullest, eat to the fullest and give themselves to the divine power of god.

This was my first answer, you need not be a saint to attain "peace", you still live the luxuries of life with the same spirit that you have while you meditate, doing what is a form of meditation but in a different costume, I need not give away every materialistic possession I wanted to have with me in order to attain my peace. Just stay and live in what you love!

I was happier with myself, forgave myself from the harsh comparisons and expectations people constantly had on me and let go myself into experimenting and rediscovering myself.

School was a great kickstart, I was back to the regular school life, though I did do home-schooling in Seychelles I hadn't missed school so much. Thanks to my mom!

Everyday seemed like a sitcom episode, every morning was a great feeling to just go to my school and be in a class where you feel, I mean in real sense the feeling of knowledge everywhere, I was witnessing a huge difference from what I learnt and witnessed in my experiences at schools in Pune, Baroda, Hyderabad and Seychelles.

I was in an International school, I was surrounded by Pakisthani's, Bangladeshi's, Sri Lankan's, Lebanese and so many different cultures. Interestingly I was able to befriend all these nationalities. I could see the huge change from a young lost girl to a more matured and easy-going person.

Though it was a mixture, I never felt exhasuted as a student to wake up to my morning alarm, it was a healthy warm morning with the recital of the Quran, as it's an Islamic country, we followed the traditions in school too.

Life seemed to have a direction, I was at terms with myself, I found myself to socialize very easily it was now my strength, I had the right amount of words in my hands to entertain people which eventually dragged them to me. It was a beginning, everything was showing up, I was doing well in academics, so well that I went to a point where I used to get one sided papers from my dad's office and make my own personal notes of every subject I studied. If this wasn't enough, my first taste to success was when I topped my class, it was a "no going back" sign, it was promising, and this went on at a stretch for 4 whole years, where I was finally into my 10 th grade.

Chapter 15

Destiny decides most of it

The fact about we Indians is, "we can leave India but India never leaves you", at least an Indian school in a parallel universe also would follow the same education system. NO MATTER WHAT!

Exactly! My point, when it came to me preparing for my boards though I was an NRI and was living in the Gulf, it never made me miss the sarcastic comments and comparisons from relatives, neighbors and possibly everyone.

So I knew the exam fever was in the air and it crossed the Arabian sea and now in my house!

The funny thing is when an Indian student is studying for her boards it's not just her but the entire family going through the curfew period.

My house was no stranger to such traditions, in fact we were disciples of this.

So, here I was burning the midnight oil. Literally till 3 am in the morning somehow or the other, battling with my eyelids. Running with my books in my hand everywhere just to keep myself awake. Everything and everyone seemed so dead in the house, though it was me who was practically going through hell. With tuitions, preparations, making rough notes, going through previous years paper, setting goals. I don't know what not, I was workaholic and at my unbelievable levels.

All those years of people telling me 10 th is the crucial time to score marks and all was in my nerves and my target was to get a 90%. Finally the day of the exam arrived.

And it was not just me going in and writing but the entire family feeling my vibes. Though I was chilled out my parents were not so easy going. My dad dropped me at the exam hall by checking if I had my hall ticket and all the needed stationary. Mom on the other side made sure there was more divine energy in me than what the breakfast could give, so prayed all day and all night. This is no different from any normal family.

Finally after a long grueling weeks of exams I was finally done with it and the results were out.

To the shock of my life I topped in social studies and scored an 87%. I was on the top of the world I felt my hard work was paid off somehow.

It was a celebration or may be a statement to "some" people that she is fit for "engineering". I know right! That's how we get labeled if we do well in academics.

It was a great summer a memorable one. All I knew was 11th standard and 12th should be more than this. I had confidence worn on my sleeve. I was in for more than my best to give for my future.

This is just a number, but if numbers were what defined your abilities are you just feel that you've received your eligibility certificate to participate in this mad race.

I was assured in a way, that I am not so bad after all.

But then it was a fashion back then when students from Gulf decide to do their higher secondary education in India or Canada. It was more like a statement which said "Now that I realized my potential, I am going for "quality education".

It was a trend or let's say a belief in most of the parents back then that their children would do wonders if sent to India.

So keeping that in mind I never backed off, I was totally in for leaving to India. I wanted to be separated from my parents, just to prove a statement that I can do bigger miracles back in my motherland.

My parents believed in my confidence more than the situations out in India. They were in one way happy and convinced that I was matured enough to take up a challenge at the age of 15 and had plans for my own future.

They never said a 'no 'to it. They felt maybe I could understand life on broader perspective.

So with all the belief, confidence and conviction my mother helped me pack my huge suitcase, my favorite novels, my personal travel diaries I maintained for the massive travelling I had done by then, starting from Seychelles, Mahe, Maldives, Sri lanka, Bahrain, Dubai, Sharjah, Abudabi.

So basically I had all my memories all my dreams packed into this huge suitcase that was going to be my partner on my journey to India all alone at 15 just to set out my self to know and tap my highest potential. All this in one way that "One number" which made me travel back to my country.

It was my decision and my parents supported. After all the packing I was at the coffee lounge with my parents and Vaibhav, waiting for my flight.

I had lots of stuff going in my mind at that point of time, the expectation was nothing compared to excitement of meeting my maternal grandmother, My aunt, my cousins Mahesh and Karan. I was closer to my mother's side more than my father's.

But above all this my heart was filled with the grief of separation from my best friend, my baby brother, my Vaibhav. I loved him more than any one on this planet. I haven't seen anything more cuter than that kid in my entire life. May be it's a sister's love for her younger brother. We were bonded for all the times that we had spent together, the shifting, the orange and mango orchards that we had been too, our life in Seychelles together in the beach, our life again in Saudi. Everytime I shifted to a new place, the only person whom I could connect my inner feelings were with vaibhav, he was there throughout my new experiences, been there in my worst times of adjusting and getting along with new people. He was a kid but he was a protective brother for me throughout my life.

It was impossible to fight my tears seeing him in the lounge with me to give me a send off.

So after all the laughing and a great chat with my dad and mom it was time for me to leave.

If I remember I was the last one to board my flight that day. I stood there, a tiny personality with huge aspirations and hopes on what's awaiting in India.

And here I was fighting hard not to break down at all, but tightly hugged my mother, with whom I spent more than anybody among the four of us considering the days my dad was in a different country when I was a kid. She was my everything. She gave me one of the massive of all the hugs she could possibly give, held me tight and gave me a huge good bye kiss. It was my brother's turn now, I was fine when mom hugged me as I felt it was an everyday thing but to the shock of my life my brother, Vaibhav finally burst out into tears, I melted to this impossible sight, I find emotions very hard to deal with I was so touched for the love he had for me.

It was impossible to bid a good bye. I couldn't stop but I was the same elder sister that I had always been, gave him a tight hug and told him how much he means to me. It was highly emotional. I was totally ok with this flow of feelings as I needed to let it out. But of all my dad was always the sweetheart of the family. He held me and just said one thing clearly "Don't lose yourself, always think of us when you do anything". That was short but it had some of the life changing events that came by from that day on.

Chapter 16

Welcome

After all the emotional goodbyes and the love I received it was time for me to leave. I was excited in one way that I am on my own, though I was financially dependent on my parents but then again I had so many dreams and fantasies being built in my head as I was heading to Hyderabad. Back to the land where I started my first journey. I had lots of things running in my mind. How my new school would be, will I bond with all my old friends Naina, Ankush, Komal and most of all Aarav. Will I meet new people, how am I going to study this time, new life, new curriculum. I was feeling responsible and more matured than any time before.

I thought "this is it". I finally landed in India.

I was a hero in my own way as it was not my parent's decision to send me to India. Out of nowhere I proposed this idea and here I was at the airport being received by my uncle and my cousin, Karan.

I was very happy to see them after all the talking and receiving I headed back to my uncles house where everyone was waiting for me. I was pleased to be welcomed, felt homely as I was very close to my aunt and grandmother I was fine, not exactly happy as I was feeling homesick. I could feel my parent's absence in spite of being with nearly 6 people in front of me.

Now that's the whole challenge it was my decision, so had to live up to it. It was nice to be around people who loved you but then I was too young to understand how to battle all the inner feelings and live with the real self that I am.

I was not sent to India to stay at my maternal grandmother's house or anywhere. I was heading to paternal grandmother's place where I was enrolled to do my 11th and 12th grade. I was never close to my father's side of the family yet I was ready to go and live here with them as my school was at this place. It was a 6 hours journey from my maternal grandmother's house.

It was a bright morning when I started off to my new location where I was starting my new chapter of life.

After a pleasant travel of 6 hours I was here at my paternal grandmothers house after about 6 years in a way. My father's mother was warm, she was happy to have her granddaughter come all the way to study in her city. She took it as a responsibility, but the fact is she was just my guardian I was here to do my 11th and 12th in a strange place which had the worst recorded summers.

I was still in my vacation, but then we got a notice from the institute that we have a one month coaching on brushing up our "basics". So, it said I followed and landed up in the institutes hostel. Right from the moment I was stepping I was with hopes that it was going to be one of those high maintained hostels, as I trusted my parents and their sensibilities on what kind of life they made me lead to what I would be comfortable when they were away from me.

I had all the highs and lows of getting along in a new place, new school and new life. It was never easy, but you just learn through the process and hold on to one or two people who genuinely love you and would want to be a part of your life. For me, this was the only pattern of growing up so far, considering my unstable life.

But then again, every new place had its own challenges to put up with and this time it was the biggest.

To the shock of my life it was nowhere close to even a common man's living conditions.

I still have no clue if my parents knew this hostel or not.

I am still taken aback by our country's education institutes, how do they even get these permissions. A hostel with 9 girls in each room with one washroom to share, a jam packed schedule from 6 in the morning to 10 in the night with just 2 hours for yourself to finish the domestic chores to eat, take a bath, get ready and even talk to your parents. A place where cellphones were not allowed only a phone booth was available which had a queue till the main entrance gate. Absolute hell!!

In my "one month" stay I hardly had a chance to speak to my mom for may be 2 times. And here I was the only NRI trying to fight through all the odds and putting up with people who had come from the interiors of Andhra Pradesh. I am no one to judge them but the thing is when you see a person who is so different from your regular set of people, you are always put at a distance from them as they find you in a way not so friendly, though your intentions would never be the way they judge you. Even the slightest difference in the kind of watch or a bangle I wore would become the subject of discussion for the day. Eventually I would be me cut from regular life and left alone to myself.

It was heating up. I had a hope and a lots of energy right from the moment I left my home in Saudi Arabia, came alone all the way with the trust in the people around me and my country's education. I can't blame the country nor myself. It was situational. I just could not get myself on track or even focus, for the constant subject of discussions not just among the student but also the teachers as they always made me feel what a mistake I did by coming here, where as I was expecting to be welcomed for a quality growth in me as a person. Expectation was my back stabber. It was an impossible stay, this institute believed in a rigid mechanism to educate their students, one way the kids here are so well prepared and polished by their mother's every week on how to face the college it never gave them a chance to see the way I was looking at it.

The subjects made no sense at all in the beginning, this was my grandmother's place which has highest recorded summers and here I am in a class filled with a 100 students who hardly know their classmates names nor do they even know their bench mates names. The day started at 7 in the morning with three hours of math, two hours of physics and 2 hours of chemistry along with it an extra three hours of studying hours, one hour for lunch so technically I spent 12 hours of my day in a factory like institute that manufactured us. Life went on in this adversity. I knew this was not the kind of thing that I had imagined over the years.

I had to find a way out, to make peace with myself. I wanted to go to mom and cry in her arms loudly but never had the chance to nor did I feel loved. It was a strange city, strange people who lived in fear of marks and exams, who had no big targets but just went with whatever they were subjected to.

I was seeing possibly something I could never imagine throughout my journey in Hyderabad, Pune, Baroda, Seychelles and Saudi Arabia.

What was even happening to me! I was not having any family member around me. I could not see a source of support or a moral energy. I was all by myself, alone and not able to understand why I was sitting in such odd conditions. I could not even explain my situations in the little time I got whenever possible to speak to my mother. My heart melted listening to her. She knew I was missing her, I was in some pain. She understood I was finding life too harsh to deal with.

It was harsh, everything I could feel or see around me was not remotely close to a normal man's living. The timings, the food I was served, the people and their thinking just did not fit me and worst of the entire climate.

This was never my upbringing as a kid, yet my relatives had so many profound opinions on my life that they made statements which were unbelievable to take in.

I could hear the people in the house talking; I was the subject of discussion for my inability to adjust to a new life without my parents support. Though people claim it as “concern” it never really touched me a bit.

I knew I was shattering inside me, I couldn’t take it anymore. I was exhausted like the time I was when I was made to change the school, back then it was parents who decided for me but now this was my decision. I had them as a source to blame but now it was all me and myself. I decided to leave Saudi Arabia, it was me who thought I would better in india and take an independent decision to start a new chapter without my parents support, yet I was unable to get along.

The lessons I was learning from my innervoice was not simple, it constantly told me the problem was not an external third person to be blamed for but it was me, my very inner me suffering. Reasons were just plastic defense materials to soak myself in a warm cocoon of sympathy the world feels for you.

I was able to hear it from the inside, I needed to hear it as all these years it was voicing out but not reacting, now was the time for reactions.

Chapter 17

Everyday Lessons!

I realized I was now in the real world and no more fantasizing of the beaches, the desserts and good old days at home.

I needed to defend myself, by defining who I am. I can't just sit around and cry all day for mom. I was this self proclaimed adult at 15 and had to live up to my image. These were my buckets of thoughts and restlessness that made me wake up every morning and control my tears and the urge to see my mom.

I held back I had to be occupied and tied to something to keep my mind focused, I was frustrated with people around me judging me all the time.

I decided to try studying day to day lesson, keep myself submerged into novels and music. I needed a way out to release these frustrations and feelings from the inside. I can't be isolated this was the phase where I needed to be in highest positive spirits to at least preserve my energy to cry my heart out when I meet my mother.

With these many lessons and thoughts in my mind I headed out to my school and one fine day, out of these many sorrowful days I couldn't find myself a bench empty to go hide myself. After scanning through the class, I found the last bench empty and picked myself out of the embarrassment of being ignored by people and walking all the way to this one last bench.

Interestingly, there was a girl who had already occupied the seat but sleeping over the bench. I hadn't seen in her class before nor did she even knew that a specimen like me existed, I was being my always good self that I put on but then thought it would be courteous to wish her a morning.

"hi, I am vidhi, sir is entering the class, I guess it's better to wake or else he may catch you sleeping"

These were my words with her.

She with her half sleep voice and an irritated look over her face just said "so what!"

"let me explain! this institute takes 12hours of your day to "polish" if your brainy enough you can manage in 6hours, so the remaining 6 hours you can have a break, so sleep now" was what she told me, on the account of just reminding that the sir had come to class.

In my first month of joining I never noticed her, but it was on this one day I accidently ended up sitting beside her and got a piece of her mind, which did make a lot of sense to me.

She was free spirited in her own way, all these days I was self-trapped in emotions, feelings and all these questioning. I saw this girl sleep at a stretch for three continuous classes beside me. Finally it was the lunch break. I was a very isolated person, I wasn't having any interest in talking to anyone as I was always put at a distance by the people here but this was one girl who seemed a little different to me.

I could not resist myself from asking her name. She is Shivani.s and her house was right beside the institute and her lunch was sent to her through the common wall which her house and the institute had shared.

"what's your problem" asked shivani.

"I am sorry, nothing. Anything wrong?" I asked.

"should I ask you to talk or will you tell me about yourself" said Shivani. Though it was a little arrogant in the beginning she has a sense of sweetness in her.

I smiled and told her 'I am Vidhi and I came from Saudi all the way hoping to do well in academics'.

She looked at me and laughed. It was a little evil laugh.

"You seem like a nice person, I don't think that nature of yours works here. My advice don't be nice, then you can do "extremely well" here "said Shivani.

Personally I was a little puzzled but then this was my new routine, every single day I used to sit beside Shivani and wake her up when the lunch bell rang and got her share of advices every lunch and that was it.

MY FIRST FRIEND IN INDIA! After my arrival.

At home I stayed with my paternal grandmother, she and I were never close, but I respected her as she was my father's mother and she was good to me as, technically I was her granddaughter my conversations with her were not much. I was given my own room which had its own entrance a cupboard, a coat and few shelves.

This room never felt like "my room" but this was my junkyard I kept all my school memories and the massive number of books and novels I had got myself to stay away from my feelings were in this room.

Every day, was something new to listen from Shivani, though half the stuff she said were very silly. Eventually we both realized how lonely we were in this institute and how badly we hated it. Time went by.

She never "ever" wrote any notes in class, she slept and I used to write it for myself.

Life was now settling down a bit, all that episodes of wanting to go home and totally different people had synced into me.

Well, we can say it was more about me learning to adjust to the fact that "life is harsh, so get used to it ".

I learnt this at a very young age, having come from a family which seems to be together and attached but never really stood by for that statement, as I could see it myself. Here I am a young girl trying to make my way out and the least anyone can give me is my space but I received a lot of opinions on what they think my decisions and life should have been.

Tired of hypocrisy and critical acclaim.

I learnt that no matter what, be it your family, friends or neighbors who you believed in will not be the same people throughout your life, it's your belief you built by the treatment you receive when you are a guest at their place but the equation is completely opposite when you starting sharing life with them.

It was a profound opening to my mind.

But then I never lost my touch with my fun and happy side. It was Shivani's presence that made a difference, we were now good friends. Things started to change a bit between us, she started to sleep less and we started to gossip more. I was getting along with the worst surroundings but a very interesting human who added life to my days.

Shivani and I shared lunch, she had been in this city all throughout her life and she started to educate me the mindset of people and how much people die for marks and status.

She was a very politically loud and opinionated person, she was silly most of the times, considering her sudden waking up and sometime blabbering and going back to sleep but I found her sensible.

She started to like me not for the baggage I came with but the person I was. She knew I was timid and I could be easily taken advantage off by people. She trusted me as a good friend and introduced me to some of her school mates who had joined this institute out of all the girls she had introduced me to there was this one girl, who was very talkative and giggled and laughed almost all the time. I personally hate girls who are girly but here she was having all the qualities I could never tolerate in a girl.

It was a brief introduction that I got from Shivani but then I wanted to know who that giggling person was, she was Seema.

Shivani had told me about her, she was never really close to her but she knew that a girl named Seema existed.

So every day I started to meet up Shivani's school friends, but most of them had their own gangs except

Seema. She was just casually hanging out possibly any of her old school friends she saw.

So, finally it so happened that Seema joined Shivani and me.

Seema, was a different person overall. She was every bit of a girl who loved pink colors and was very religious with her sense of style and dressing.

She had a persona that had energy and intimidated people at times, but it never gave any one a chance to give up on themselves.

She was a little loud in her outfits, she was easily judged to be a person with huge attitude problems or may be some term it as arrogance. But honestly to the person I was all I could see and pick from her was her "confidence".

It's sad that many people judge each other based on the outfits and the grace with which one carries herself. The fact is real world wants exactly this kind of people, a plain Jane is not a symbolism for being humble and modest, it just shows a lack of confidence when you try to imitate the crowd.

But Seema, was exactly opposite to this, she radiated tons of positive energy, where as Shivani was more realistic, though she appeared lazy and had loud arrogant opinions on the system of education, the institute and the faculty. She knew it somewhere in the back of her head that it's simply her ranting that made her feel better but she was sure no big changes would actually happen in a factory like living conditions.

So this was the three of us Shivani the real one, Seema the confident loud one and myself, Vidhi …well! Let's say my identity was mostly a confused one but definitely the calm one out of those two.

Chapter 18

A new world

We three bonded in a very short span of time and now I had a permanent bench in my class of 100 people. Yes! you read it right it was more like the animals gracing in a closed room than going and studying.

Finally, I was saved from the daily embarrassments of facing everyone as I walked in search of an empty space just to fit in with anyone possible for that one day.

I too had two new friends and I too had my very own bench! This was just a tiny rush of confidence that 'I will be fine', nothing to cry much on.

Seema and Shivani used to sit beside me, we were three girls who absolutely hated the entire idea of an institute like this one.

I know I joined with this "crazy intention" on what it's like to be on my own in India but Shivani and Seema had totally different stories. It was always a doubt for me as to why a girl like Seema was sitting in a class with nerve wrecking subjects.

and lessons in physics, chemistry and math.

It was a worst academic planning I have ever come across out of the many schools I had been to. All the initial feelings of loneliness and not given importance started to subside a bit or I can say, I was safely in the company of two amazing girls who made me forget my deep pains.

The class liked us now, though initially Seema and I were always judged to be loud and girls with attitude, we were loved by almost everyone who spoke to us.

I felt girly around Seema as she had this artistic approach to life, anything she wore or spoke about had something to do with being extrovertly creative and unique.

Shivani was more of life and the consequences that need to be thought off, as she lived a little practically. What I really loved about her was she never ever got carried away with the girly possession that were in the market or that was with everyone, she was absolutely herself, totally thrown back, happy, easy going attitude with a tough exterior.

Life was showing up now, all the crying and missing my mother started to vanish.

Well, I was growing up, learning to live on my own.

But then again I kept questioning myself if all this was happening for real and also the fear of 'this can't be permanent' always kept me grounded with my feelings.

We three were like sisters, whatever we achieved or devastated was a total threesome and this time it was the exams time. I was absolutely clueless as to what I was going to do in the exam hall or possibly it was a question of how would I kill those three hours.

"I haven't studied a word, I am going to Vidhi's place, you better come or else we are never going to pass" this was Seema's idea. Well, it was more like a warning notice.

Fact is of all three I was a little sincere compared to the two of them. So she had a bit of hope that if we three did a combined study, we can pull off something.

So as per the plan, we all crashed at my place. As I stayed with my father's mother, my grandmother was a very courteous person when it came to me and some of the new people I had in my life at that point of time. Though I was not much connected to her she showed her care very often. Her house was huge, my grandfather passed away when I was about two years old, I hardly have any of his memories with me. So this house was basically grandmom and I with a few servants who took care of the garden and the household chores. So as such there was no entertainment or distraction. And Seema being the smart one picked my house for this sole reason.

It was perfect. Starting from that day the next 20 days were our preparation season and we had to do something as we hardly listened to any of the classes, though we used to write notes in class, but that was just a way to keep ourselves awake and sometimes to see how neatly we could write.

But then we had no choice and absolutely no where to go or get rid of these exams.

So finally with all the strategies and ideas we all met at my house and started the "rigorous" preparation. My room had a separate entrance which had its own balcony. It was more like a separate house and no one really disturbed or called for us as we used to step out of the room just for lunch or may be some water.

We pushed the cot in my room to one side and swept the floor neatly and laid all the books and the syllabus sheets and started to go through.

We wanted to get a picture of what exactly we were studying in our institute. The funny thing is, we never thought of this for any of the exams that passed by during the entire year, since this was my final exam in my 11th grade we had no choice but to study.

After all the searching and sorting we found that we have no clue on any of the lessons they had taught in class.

We were so fed up with our situation that whatever arrangement we had made on the floor finally ended up in sleeping for about two hours.

It was just insane. It just hit us badly, how lethargic we were. The fact is none of our parents pressurized us on the importance of studying everyday or we never had the fears like the other kids had in class regarding marks and percentage. We were constantly compared, at least I was compared, which just used to make me loose the last bit of interest that was left within but never was I told or given an awareness of what is all this 11th and 12th for. How's life going to change with what we take up as our degree or how important it is to know what we like.

Nothing of this sort was ever spoken about among us three or at least in the house.

After sleeping for about two hours, finally we were awake and this time we had to hit it, hit it so hard that we finish the target and make sure we know what we were studying and also be in par with our classmates.

Starting from that very moment Seema, Shivani and I were deeply committed to the routine of understanding the whole lesson and making notes and started to explain each other.

This was the only way out.

It was a huge process with loads of night outs and cutting away all the talking and gossips we were late up all night learning and practicing all the portions

Until the final exam.

Final exams were fast approaching we three somehow managed to come to an average level of preparation, with all the massive night outs, arguing and discussing and sometimes just throwing away everything and gossiping, with all the drama and energy we were able to feel a ray of hope. But it was not sufficient. Shivani was always cribbing about how we hadn't done much of the syllabus the way it was meant to be, until one fine morning she just came to us with a huge grin and said

"I found us a tutor, from now on I'll take tuitions and then teach you both properly".

We were stunned, why! because this was never us!

She went an extra mile not just for herself but for us too. I was not happy or even upset but I was really confused to see a person like this. She just randomly comes on a fine day just to say she found us a tutor and she was going to help us out by taking lessons under him. For a second I was speechless. And it was solely because of her that we managed to face our exams successfully.

It was genuinely touching and felt so warm after such a long time of my arrival in India.

I understood how much we both meant to her. We were so happy on that one fine day that we hugged each other so tight, my very first hug after an entire year in India, with two of the most amazing people I loved the most.

My life was changing, all the years of travelling my time with my other friends Naina, Aarav, Ankush and many more now were memories. Somewhere deep down I always had the thoughts of what it would be like if I could meet them again or where could they possibly be staying now or do they remember me. There were massive thoughts if any of them remembered me or at least the only person I was closet to in my schooling was Aarav, I wasn't even sure where is he from. All I know was his name, no clue about him as a person or anything. Naina, was one of the sweetest girls I had as a friend but I was curious to know about these two people the most at that point.

Though Seema and Shivani were my world, there was a parallel search for these two people almost on a daily basis.

I had no access to internet, the maximum I had access to was a landline phone where I received only calls from parents, Seema and Shivani.

But every bit of a chance or an access to internet I used to search for them on FaceBook, Orkut, Linked In, possibly everything. I don't know why this search, but all I knew was I badly wanted to reconnect with my childhood and spend that remaining time with them, which I couldn't as I was always been put in a new place or a new school every time I made peace with myself and a made a life for myself. I did not have the slightest bit of loosing people whom I met, who made a difference in my personality under any cost and this search was just for the same reason.

My present was setting up, academically I was struggling to cop up with my basics and this factory like institute but then I had a family here.

All the emotional stress of not seeing my parents and being with a person whom I wasn't really connected to and actually listening to a society's outrageous comments on "today's generation" without knowing each of our stories was finally showing a path of hope.

Shivani and Seema were like my lost sisters and still are, our days mostly started with phone calls on who is wearing what to the class today and once we met up our trash talk would range from the latest political happenings in the country to family issues, different ways to improvise this god forsaken institute and what education should be like to what we really think we should do as a career.

Chapter 19

Twists and Turns

Finally, after a year struggle at home with relatives and my feelings, I was setting myself into a normal routine. Eventually it was very hard, as I always had to put up with uninvited guests who spoke about the greatness of some relative in their house who made it through IIT or Bits or some flashy engineering college.

Most of the time, it was just free advices I got from people on the importance of deciding "now". I still don't get it. People enjoy lecture and advices when it comes to giving them for free to others. All that went in my mind while they gave their speech was this "Yeah! like Whatever.. if u leave now I can sleep".

It was sheer arrogance and exhaustion of some random person who don't know me, my story, my baggage coming one fine morning just as a guest and giving me free lessons on 'my life'.

I had no choice but to listen.

My life was more realistic. There were truckloads of experiences which needed to be written down somewhere, so deep and so loud. It was a daily thing, tolerance was my new armor, as kids it is ignorance that protects you but tolerance taught me patience and patience made me calm from the inside.

I knew I was still a puppet in every ones hand except that I had a long rope tied to me from my parents, family and neighbors.

I had a lot of questions left within me to wake me up.

I was deeply broken down inside as a kid to my adolescence I was told by some outsider or the other on how to live peacefully, how to set targets, how to be successful, how to run in this race for getting a good seat. Everything I was told never really registered in my head as I knew I could not implement somebody's else's brains or ideas.

I knew I was never going to fulfill somebody's wishes considering the state of mind I had been all these years.

I looked for liberation.

Liberation in thoughts, my own 2 millimeter radius that need not make me go around with slogans on what I am or who I am or what I feel life should be like.

It was crazy mess, having to deal the inner person that you are and be a social animal with all the respect and virtues. For me social life was a nerve wrecking problem though I was my highest best in showering unwanted respects to people who have a loud mouth to give opinions and suggestions on my life which was clearly not out of love or care but just a statement to say how they have made their life from boring to somewhat sucking by these advices, out of joblessness, it was not easy to be myself, I could never be myself.

Most of the times I feared judgment and critical acclaim from people for being what I am, though I was told life was about choices. My choices were also given by the world but never by me.

I struggled a lot to be the person I wanted to be, but I wasn't aware of what I really wanted to be!

It was a year, my 12th grade finally was also over, Seema and Shivani were holidaying at their place where as I finally went to Saudi to visit my parents.

It was two year after I had shifted to India, coming back home was bliss, I was exhausted from the inside.

I was finally, heading back to Saudi for a vacation.

It was a very special home coming as my brother, Vaibhav was looking forward to see me.

We were away from each other for an entire year, to come back seemed lot more exciting considering all the gossips and fun we both missed out on.

After a pleasant 4 hours flight, I was back to the "CamelLand". I was finding my own house a little new. The roads and the shopping malls everywhere seemed something fresh and it was more like I never lived in this luxury.

These were going in my head.

Heading home, I could see my mother waiting for me, finally I was welcomed with a tight hug and all of us were emotional to meet everyone after so long.

It was amazing to come back, but then it was my time to decide on what I wish to do as my degree.

My mom did not really give me a choice as I was exempted from taking up an IIT coaching and also we learnt later that Mrs. Gajapathi aunty's daughter did not make it to IIT. My mom, eventually understood that coaching would not be the key to crack a seat in IIT, but she was very clear that it was engineering that I was born and meant to do.

'Impossible'

Was the word going in my head, it was not easy to convince my mom that there are other better degrees which I could easily crack.

But it never occurred to me as to "what is it that I want to do!" or "why is it that I found engineering to be not such a big deal".

It was not easy, as I myself had no answer, no awareness or no expectations on future.

But I was always told from the beginning that "life is all about your choices". Well! Not anymore, it was about choices but always a third person's and never mine.

It was a battle within me, for myself understanding what is to be done was just out of my hands.

These decisions were never mine, the only time I took charge of what I decided I fixed it myself, it was the moment I decided to move to India, but this idea of doing engineering was not in my hands at all. I was not aware of what it meant or what would it lead me, what are the good colleges for it or what is the life of an engineer. Nothing at all, fact is my parents were also not aware. But it was a society thing, it was what the market demanded or labeled it at a safe career to get a good savings account.

But the truth not every engineer is a good engineer.

Well, this one vacation went away in me being brainwashed on this subject. I tried hard I digested. My life was clearly not in my control.

I was vexed.

But then on the brighter side I had a hope as I could see Shivani going through the same process as I did. I never felt lonely when it came to the discussion on being forcefully doing engineering. I could relate my irritation with Shivani.

On the other end, Seema was having her share of troubles, though she was given her liberty to choose any degree she wished to. It was still not easy for her as we were three girls with skills but no marks. The world demands numbers but not quality, we knew we had the personality in us which was influential but we were unaware on how markets or institutes run only on numbers.

It was one period of time, I had to start penning down every bit of the noises my inner voice made to calm myself down.

My journal was my god, when no one listened only the white paper listened to every bit of sorrow of having to do what everyone advices and suggests.

There was also this thought at times where I felt, "If only, I knew what I am good at or I knew what I am searching for "…ahh!when will I get over my grief!.

It was a routine where I had arguments, discussions and digesting all the talk over the phone with my parents and crying out all the irritations near Shivani, every single day and penning it all down in my journal, just to see what exactly I was feeling to at least try analyzing myself.

But something strange happened on a fine day.

Chapter 20

Reality check

It was not as harsh as it seemed like. The issue was just a massive competition and the love of parents over their children that never let them made me do anything risky. Fair from their point of view but I wasn't prepared to face engineering, like most of the kids who hate to be in one of these over rated institutes.

I needed to calm myself down, put away these thoughts from me and I kept myself occupied by journaling down all the raising questions in me, my time with some of the most amazing people shaped me as a person. Topics related to existence, fantasies of a parallel world with an adventurous life and many more. I was lonelier and cut from everything around me when I was journaling down all this. But then again I never stopped hanging out with Seema and Shivani.

They were my pillars, they lived with me in every situation possible. It was a bond, an unbreakable bond of friendship. But then again the search for two of the most important people in my life never ended, Naina and Aarav. Though I kept searching for them every single time and place, I used to ask a lot of common friends and strangers whom I never met or who knew me about me. But it was never ending search for them.

They were just friends to me, but it was a chance to rewind and live those days of school with Naina and those moments I shared with Aarav in my most lonely time in a world of complete opinions and reviews.

Though I was back from my vacation I was still in a holiday with Seema, Shivani was at her grandmother's place. It so happened that for the first time Seema wanted to know me more at a deeper perspective.

"I know you for two years but I really don't know much about you, what was your life like before you landed here, ' Seema asked this question out of strange curiosity. She knew that I wasn't here just for doing my 11th and 12th grade, but my mind had something big planned for, when I came here.

"That's a strange question you have ever asked me" I laughed and replied "I don't know may be to meet you both or may be to just be realistic ".

"umm….I am not convinced, Vidhi. I see you every single day and had been seeing you every single day from two years, we gossip, we shop around, we eat together, we study together but there is something you are always so secretive about."

"Secretive! well I don't know I had been to 6 different places and 6 different environments with too many people in my life I loved and now I am in a search of them" is what I said to her, as it was a fact and one of my very reasons to come to India as, all I wanted was a reconnection with the people who been there with me and made the person I was at that point of time and the inner quest to really find the true person I was.

"Really! You never told me this story at all. All I knew about you was this NRI who just laughs and has fun with me all the time, I am curious to know all these people who are in search of" said Seema with a little stunned voice and a lot of curiosity.

"I am searching for my two best friends from school Aarav and Naina, I met them in school, it may sound silly but I don't know why I have these insane anxieties inside of me to find where they are and again relive the moments I had with them" I replied Seema, she was listening to me.

"Do you have any idea about Aarav?" Seema asked me in her detective tone, "I love him as my best friend but it never felt in a romantic way or flirtatious way, as he was this random person who was selflessly trying to get me along with the flow of my schooling days, I don't know what he would get out of it but it just seemed weird all the time and the thought of it makes me curious as to what was it between Naina and Aarav, though I met them in different schools. They just kept me happy." I replied to Seema as she was restless now and she was also ready to listen

"Vid! I love you tons, but don't waste your happiness and energy for something which was an old chapter" said Seema looking straight into my eyes.

It made absolute sense it was an old chapter, does it bother everyone! Not really! Then why waste my energy, I had a huge life in front of me to enjoy, learn and grow. It was making sense, considering my hatred towards engineering started to mellow down too. I tried and tried and tried to come in terms with the truth of never finding all the people I met and the truth of doing engineering under any cost.

"Do you know, how brainy you sound to me at times" I told Seema and she started laughing.

This my last day with Seema and Shivani we were heading to our respective colleges. We three were now moving out to three different cities Shivani was going to Hyderabad, Seema was leaving to pursue her passion in design at a university in Coimbatore and I was leaving to Kerala for my engineering.

Last day, was not in the mainstream way where we hug and cry but it was very matured and different. We knew we had to depart, but we knew we were three lost sisters who can never be broken. The invisible ropes of love never broke between us but it was just a matter of career and the truth had to be digested.

And here we are off to our places. It was a reality and had to be tested.

To everyone's surprise

I was off to Tamil Nadu, by destiny or force to begin my engineering.

Chapter 21

Degree Drama

Honestly, I was ok with staying in Kerala as long as I wasn't near another annoying neighbor, who never really gives you a choice to even think and corrupts your parents mind. I was fine, I wanted to be away. Also I always felt I may meet up all my old friends and new relations would build up, maybe it was all in my fantasy world but I was in peace when I dreamt so.

All those thoughts of how would it be if we accidently bumped into each other! Or how about I meet Aarav and Naina as my bench mates and suddenly realize our childhood bond together, however cinematic it was I always had it fancied in my head.

Well, first day of engineering my parents came by to drop me and just wanted to make sure I was put safely in the hostel, for most kids it was a jail from their "happy free life and easy going" attitude as this was one place where life was more 'restricted' according to them. Though I found a certain freedom, in this restriction and a choice decided by parents, I was now finding a space for myself.

I felt like a new life, I was completely away from any family member I knew. It was perfect timing to evolve and grow as I had no support from anybody, I was now able to be somehow independent in terms of taking care of myself, the choice of food, the setting of alarm, these were the smallest unnoticed things but they were the most vital parts of my day which were managed away by either my mother or my grandmother when I moved to India.

This new found independence showed me a picture of the real self that I am, I was able to see my inner self and specially made me understand how well I am in my organizational skills. It was actually learning experience where you wake up to your own alarm call, rush to the washroom just to catch a washroom for a peaceful bath as you have the fear of someone else who might occupy it. It was all about me and my moves, no one to blame or no one to even take the blames.

Life was not easy this 'taking care of the self' was in a way making me harmonious in my approach with people as we all were away from our families, even though we hated or loved each other we had to be there in our outmost diplomatic self if we were to pull off this degree peacefully.

I was liking this place for the fact that it was making feel my existence, though the other inmates constantly cribbed about the lunch and the dinners served here and the lectures and the distance they had to walk inside the campus. It never felt that way to me as I felt like I was released from the jail of "consciousness" to an open arena but it had a compound wall called the 'engineering wall'.

I never liked it at all, I in fact hated being in the classroom so much that I felt restless every single day, every second I sat there felt like I was in the middle of a dessert however cool the breeze around me was. I tried to battle inside myself to calm down, I tried my best I kept telling myself "it's not so bad, I can do this" I knew the harsh truth was I couldn't. But the question was, was I able to live with this truth inside of me? Well, never.

I had to make peace with myself. I had to save me from my very own self it was sometimes as though a hand full of sand was slipping off between my fingers and the other sides. I was dealing with myself, I had so much to repair within myself, where was the question of going around saving the world and selflessly helping others!

This was my state in my degree time, I was able to mingle, be courteous to people and everything but this inner noise could never be heard. It was a silent war inside myself, this was never new to me, this is what I had lived with throughout.

The issue initially was the massive questions that kept rising in me but now I just found my solution, I just needed to keep these questions at peace for that I needed an answer, every time I came across different people it just felt like I was unwrapping the answers one by one.

I know engineering was not my cup of tea, but does it mean I get the liberty to leave it right away and do what I feel like? Obviously, no! As I had to answer my parents at least if not the society, on what I intend to do when I still have no clarity on what I am searching for.

Amidst all these, I was making new friends around again as always and somehow my class became a mini gang. It was a nice feeling to find people from different states meeting up in this one class. It's degree, these friends were definitely not for life but I can safely say they were worthy enough to exchange class lecture notes and materials. But then again it was not for life but based on availability and the need with which these strings were attached.

I call them simple business relationships, which is not even remotely close to friendships. I was getting to learn the importance of not being close yet being in the limits that need not involve too much of the self, some call it selfishness, but then I call it "I am too busy with the inner battle".

But then I don't know how, but I remember this one time where the whole class had planned a trip to a nearby place to visit a beach, though it was during one of the weekends, I was also ready to leave as it was away from Kerala, though we had gone for the fun aspect I wasn't really looking forward for any fun or anything I just wanted to click pictures and see the place around and may be write a little bit on my experience on going to this new place.

As planned we all left from the hostels and reached this place we all dispersed with our respective gang of friends I never had a huge bunch of friends so I was on my own, I felt like exploring around this new place. I walked through this new place, I have read a lot about this place which was near the Tamil Nadu region. I reached this one part of the city which had a huge board stating "Ashram and heritage center".

I did not understand what exactly it was about. I was aimlessly walking through, but then it was allowed to all age groups. I just walked in and there was a tall man in his 40's who smiled at me and asked "how can I help you? Dear"

I did not know what exactly was happening here, but the man had a little badge with his name on it in bold letter's which said Dr. Agarwal. He was sitting in a small room near the entrance and was escorting all the visitors and patiently solving everyone's queries.

I went to him and asked "What is this center about, I just walked in seeing the board outside"

Dr. Agarwal looked at me and smiled "well, I would suggest you to walk straight and take left, where you will come across a huge hall, you will get your answer there, my dear."

I was curious, but I was running out of time as we all had to go back to college before sunset. Dr. Agarwal was a tall man, with a clean shave and his face had a childlike appearance. He seemed to be a calm person but his smile was the most beautiful of all. He directed me to go to a hall, which had a magnificent dais which was filled with flowers from possibly all over the world.

It was a flowery carpet, it was covered in bands of yellow, green and pink where as the ceiling was a rainbow pattern of flowers. It was beautiful, there were lamps lit around the entire place, the hall had an aroma of sandal wood spreading around. But then it was filled with about 5000 people from different nationalities sitting over the floor. I went in, thought of was sitting in the backside, it was filled with people from Japan, Indonesia, Venezuela and Poland. Everyone had a tiny book in their hand which had the Veda's written in their respective languages, it was an ashram but more of a recreational and selfless organization. It had positive vibes all around. I do not know how destiny plays around at times, but this one incident was a game changer!

After everyone had settled down, one of the group sitting in the front of the row picked up the mike and started to chant the Veda's. To my utter astonishment it was unbelievable, they sang in a loud tempo in chorus yet very melodiously. It was just so energetic to mingle and sing, I knew nobody nor did I have an idea on what this place is all about and what service activities take place here, I was blindly following the crowd but loving every bit of what I was doing. It was an energetic flow of slokah's I was feeling extremely happy from the inside, it was the energy around me that actually made me feel the happiness flowing through me and my veins. It was a message from heaven's or more like a call from the lands far away. It was a matter of 20 mins, I realized I was praying so happily and actually listening to my inner self and the energy that was flowing through me in that hall. But then I had to leave to my hostel as it was time and we were not allowed to stay in the city for long.

That night I lay down in the bed thinking of the joy and happiness I felt through myself when I was sitting in that prayer hall. I could understand how powerful those vibes were and I was more connected to my higher self. I was deeply feeling grateful to Dr. Agarwal I was really feeling grateful to this man. Though I still did not know what this place was about I was feeling a lot calmer inside.

My classes seemed to be better now as it was always the counting in my head for the weekend so that I could just go to this center and explore the other things around the place. I wanted to know what else they teach or what exactly they do.

Chapter 22

Weekends

Finally, the weekend had come by now I was also free from my exams and preparations. I was not so good at my engineering subjects but I managed. Though I was doing injustice to myself by doing something which I could not justify, destiny never let me go free on that aspect, instead gave me new routes. Though it was our semester leave everyone were heading to their house to meet their parents and here I was heading to the "Ashram". Well, first thing is my parents did not stay in India and I wasn't close to any of my family members, moreover I did not want to be on any one's help and support.

I was heading to this 'Ashram'. I had finally arrived to the place where I spotted Dr. Agarwal with his calm composed smile. I think he recognized me well, he asked "so I see again here?" I was quick to answer as I wanted to thank him and tell him how I felt "yes sir I felt good, I want to thank you for sending me into that hall"

"Oh! don't thank me, thank the guru it's your destiny and the guru's choice that brings you here more often than you think" said Dr. Agarwal with his smile and welcoming attitude. I liked his company very much though he spoke very little he always enjoyed me coming over and over again.

This was my routine, I used to attend classes regularly just to treat myself in this ashram with the daily prayer and meet Dr. Agarwal and have a healthy happy conversation with him.

The guru was never present physically but then the people behaved with utmost respect and love towards each other.

"Dr. Agarwal why is it that the guru never comes to meet us" I asked, as I have never seen the guru in my many of my visits to the ashram.

With a smile he started to talk to me "guru is everywhere, all you need to do is listen to the inner voice that has been irritating you, it will guide you through and you will be your own life coach, it's sad that our education in India is not nurturing this among most of you all, I wish it was implemented and taught on mastering the self with the voice that guides you through, I really wish, anyways it's too late" said Dr. Agarwal.

He was a very intelligent father like person I ever met, I shared a lot of my inner most doubts on existence and incarnation and the inner energy. It was not just me but there were times when my two best friends Seema and Shivani dropped by to meet me in my university days, got a chance to meet Dr. Agarwal as well.

He was a very patient man in his 50's, his day started at 4.45 am with a calm prayer, some light music, a cup of tea and some journaling. I don't know what he used keep working on but he had a studio filled with photographs of a person, who would be around 17-18 years old. I don't know Dr. Agarwal beyond the fact that I used to share my thoughts on the education systems and his thoughts on what's it like to live a happy life.

But his studio was mysterious he seemed to have a past which I was initially not curious about. The pictures he had in his studio were some of the best forms of photography. I assumed him to be a photographer but always wondered if he was a doctor considering his name. I never asked nor did that discussion ever come, but I respected him like my father. He was a mentor to me in every aspect. I looked up to him and his take on life, more like a role model he was a very enthusiastic man whose energy could be felt and made me always feel like doing something beyond my capabilities. He knows my baggage and my experiences of being victimized in a society filled with hypocrisy and a choice. We connected on this particular topic, very much, though he was nearly 25 years older than me.

Life went on, infact this was the little world I had created in order to get over myself from all the drama. This was a new channel to a new chapter.

Until one day

It was my 4th year into engineering I was caught up in my exams and hostel life and my hunt for a job, as it was my time to finally settle down with a job at least for the neighbors and the society to not come and bug my parents with questions on where I am working! Or what am I upto in my life! I found that very daunting, when it is my life when I am struggling my ways out to deal with it how can anyone come and give their 'over imaginary 'opinions.

And this time it was no excuse, to hardest of moments to deal with comparisons I never found the way to properly channelize it.

It was everyone's decision and choice on the kind of degree I had to do, but I was always told life is a choice!

Dr. Agarwal was a very influential character in my life, I had become a volunteer at this ashram. Though I wasn't involved in social work I had a very soft and better understanding on what goes with in the ashram.

With my occasional visits to his studio, for his inspiring photography, though I still wondered who was this young boy he clicked pictures of. I wanted to spend as much time as I could at the ashram for the massive lessons that were everywhere in the environment, but I couldn't have this liberty. It was my final year of engineering and a crucial period to deal with.

I somehow with whatever possibilities I can, I finished my degree. But now was the biggest question "where did I get my first job?". This is where the difference had come, everyone around me was an engineer but the question was how good are they and how many made it through the job hunt?

Fact is, it was an open secret. The daunting nature of the society does not let you be the 'real you'. The 'real me' never wanted engineering, but never knew what it wanted either and now comes the question of finding myself a job.

More than anything it was the stress of what would my parents answer the people. I hated this thought how much ever I avoided but it looked me into my face all the time.

I was exhausted mentally, is there an end to this? the world is not so gracious to give you a chance just because you couldn't secure what ten others are able to at the same age, but my question inside of me was do they realize that I have been given my own name and I ought to have my own identity as well!

I learnt and understood this at a very young age and it was coming all over again.

Chapter 23

Back into Time

The time with Mrs. Gajapati Pillai, I felt like a ignition less machine, which had no more fuel in it, to process criticism. I was very much a human and tears did come out profusely but that wasn't the solution, self sympathy was just escapism. I had to bring out that "something "which I wasn't able to reach out for many years now.

I was searching jobs everywhere, possibly every single website and place I could go, I was on the look out. A time when I understood how unemployment feels and how important it is to respect any sort of a profession. It was never a question of big or small but it was about sustaining in it how much ever you hated it or were not satisfied.

Amidst all this, I never stopped journaling my feelings in my journals that I had been writing over the years. It saved me from me. It kept my thoughts in a frame and made me view the picture as a third person.

This was an ongoing process. Those journals kept piling all day. I don't know what I was up to, I was at my home back in Hyderabad but it felt special only on the first day but it never really felt welcoming, as the question of where and what I am upto in life never hid behind me. It was there and looking me straight into my eyes. Accomplishments were what people demanded.

My frequent visits to the ashram taught me the art of handling my feelings and the basics of humanity, because this was one place that dealt with people with huge emotional baggage and the essence of humanity lies in feeling their pain and stepping into their shoes and seeing the world through their eyes.

In this process I understood the lengths I could go to when I was managing the simple tasks I was assigned, I thoroughly enjoyed every moment of selfless service made me connect. My income was the one smile and satisfaction the inmate got through our service, it cannot replace even if I had a fat pay check in a high end job.

Dr. Agarwal was the head of the management, after a lot of hesitation I couldn't control and asked him his story. It was not a pleasant one he was from New Zealand, a neuro surgeon and a widower and it was after his love passed away he decided to give up his practice for a selfless existence and built this center where people from different parts of the world came over and were healed mentally and emotionally.

For me, this man was a life coach. Everyone finds their reference points, who are in the form of guru's, parents or friends but for me it was Dr. Agarwal. I found the coach of my life, I don't mean to say I was dependent or he was my brain but he was a ray of light in the darkest of moments to guide me through the driest and untouched corners of life.

The idea here was very simple, you serve others to serve yourself. I used to help the people around with the online registrations and arrangements for incoming participants for various events the ashram organized on a monthly basis.

This was a life I had chosen while I was doing my engineering, simultaneously.

Having considered the worst times of judgments by relatives and neighbors on what they assumed to be my side of the story.

Everyone has their own explanations, every critic tried to bring a 'change ' in someone else's life is through judgment but not with sensitivity. People want a chance to vent out their anger on someone who is in the process of "trying" which is cruel. I personally felt it every second when I was asked what I wished to do with my life. Or how can you just get a 60 percent mark? How can you not plan your life? These questions were haunting everywhere be it in any language, be it sarcastically, emotionally or angrily these questions never left me.

I was deeply upset, these situations kept coming all throughout not just at this point of time but almost at every stage. I had tears that waited to burst out but no one around to bring it out on. But I was a little calmer inside as it was time to go back to my hostel and vacate my hostel, as decided I was in my train. It was a long 18 hours travel, a peaceful journey, I guess I just slept all throughout the journey not thinking anymore.

I was finally in my hostel room tired of this huge journey, but to add a little sweetness to this peaceful journey a note which looked like a medical prescription was pasted over my wall.

It said:

"Parent's can never be your armors as long as you don't tell them what your armor is. Your plan B is your best friend that stands by you. The point where you're inner strength and your inner energy were tapped is where you ought to be.

I have a surprise waiting for you

- Dr. Agarwal"

This was the note I read the moment I stepped into my room. It was very endearing to have a person at times like these. I felt good seeing this. I rushed to the ashram, for some reason I felt there was an answer waiting for me there.

"Hi, I need to meet Dr. agarwal" I was anxious to see him and so I asked the receptionist.

"Oh! He is waiting for you in his studio "the young lady said it with a smile.

I started to walk really fast. I had tons of thoughts hovering in my mind like a honey bee comb, most of them were on the fact of departing, it feels like dejavous all over again. This is hard to start a fresh beginning. The only thing that kept running through my head as I was rushing to meet Dr. Agarwal was "nothing is permanent and nothing remains with you ". These words were just harsh truths, may be they are negative but they were harsh.

All throughout my life it was somebody's decision but not what I wished to become. And now it's inevitable truth and harsh reality to leave a place where I found my peace.

I was lost.

"Vidhi! Welcome my dear "said Dr. Agarwal, surprised to see me upset and he knew every bit of my grief and the pain of living a world of hypocrisy.

"I just … I just came" I was stammering. And here was this man smiling at me and said "Vidhi, meet my son Aarav".

Stunned and frozen in my thoughts.

What do I utter? I was so dumbstruck for a moment.

"Aarav! You mean my schoolmate Aarav! The guy who always wanted me to talk "I said with the most shocked and lost tone I ever spoke in.

All those tears and pain and the entire journey's exhaustion just vanished away. I did not know when all this meeting up and talking about me happened I was curious.

It was a delightful moment to reunite, though these people were not my family, they were much more than that I was still digesting this surprise. Was so happy with this meet that I broke into tears and hugged Dr. Agarwal and Aarav.

I was uncontrollable I don't why I started to cry this badly. Though I always dealt with myself in my head I wasn't able to control this time. I tried to sooth myself but I was not able to.

I needed to let it out.

"My dear I know your pain, I understand your anguish but I know more than what you know about yourself. Your strength can never cheat you or hide from you for long. I have read all your eight journals, I did not know your emotional and your travel stories I understand your pain of helplessness when the world expects you to be your highest best and criticize even though you try, but what you have been missing out is the fact that you have to build a plan B, this is going to be your light of hope and a best friend" said Dr. James in this meet which for some reason hit me straight into my brain.

It was making sense; I was trying hard to be with the crowd following them, because apparently someone's success route is sealed as your success story too.

But all that I missed out was I was journaling down all these experiences of not able to become the sarcastically told statement by the people "You Can Become Anything You want". How foolish of my mind! I was told I could become anything and life was a choice but then the crowd and the neighbors, in fact also hadn't given me a second to give it a thought. As I thought over, it just felt like an excuse I searched to calm myself from the fear of facing guilt.

My plan B was right in front of me, I had the choice to work on my eight journals, these were the eight beautiful stories of my time at my ancestral home, My time with Naina, My time in the forests of Gujarat, My bundle of joy I felt in the morning prayers at Pune, the island life at Seychelles, the Arab days in Saudi Arabia, my return to India and finally meeting Dr. Agarwal.

I had it right in front of me, to choose or not to choose was my choice, since they said, that I could become anything I wanted I made up my mind to publish.

Chapter 24

The opening of a new chapter

I realized my dream of happiness was right in front of me. I was with Aarav and Dr. Agarwal right there in the studio. That day was the most defining day of my life I was feeling hopeful for what I was dealing with until then.

I was stronger than before, my journals made me feel like a wakeup call.

That one night's decision on what I wished to do with myself and the plan B, brought in me my highest disciplined self as this was the choice I took for myself and was not one of those neighbor's who always planned for me.

In one way journaling down went on in a more rapid phase. The thing is once you realize what you want to do with your life and your dream is realized all the excuses and reasons seem like a poor man's act.

I wanted to go to my highest best in this, the next one year all I did was editing proof reading developing and researching for publishing my journals.

It went on. Everyday seemed like a meditation, the work I was submerging myself into never felt like work, it was like a normal life where you have the sense of peace developing in you.

I was connecting with myself, I could hear the answers I had wanted and was in search of for what I was up to. I now realized this is what I was meant for, I was deeply thanking inside of me for all the people who came into my life as hypocrites, who judged me, compared me and mocked me at the end for my inability. It all made sense now, I needed all of them. It was them and their cynical hollow comments that ripped my soul to search the real person I was looking for in me.

I was analyzing my journey as a third person, viewed these frames in my life as a movie. It had every bit of the flavor a movie needs. I was feeling eternally happy. It was a rear form of happiness which is undisturbed with the external chaos, something that stays still and stationary. It was at its highest forms, which was radiating my energy's.

I was feeling powerful from the inside, it was the feeling of how beautiful life has been and how my story has been shaped into.

I was able to compile my 8 journals with sincerity. I saw them as an energy that made me write, never did I believe it was me who came up with that piece of work.

Finally, it was Dr. Agarwal and Aarav who got the 1st out of the 8 journals to be published.

I never thought these two people would be a part of my story, they stood by me.

I was not sure of its out come.

They were more confident than I was, as they felt like an untold feelings of the human behavior but I always felt it to be a natural flow, which any random person felt.

The following six months was a life changing moment. I was able to make a tiny mark in this ocean.

There were around 28,000 followers for this journal. The journal was published in the form of parts.

I was surprised to notice the reader's curiosity as it felt impossible for me. I was termed as a "WRITER".

I was no more the lost engineer, without a job. It was an identity which I never searched for, it came searching for me.

It was this one title, that made all the difference.

So much that, people's curiosity made me want to write more, initially no one understood why I used to publish these journals and it looked odd.

But as people started to read they were connecting with their lost self's and the sarcasm that we live in, "you can become anything you want" this was my theme.

I wanted to unleash the truth of how to become whatever we wanted by first doing what others wanted, be it our parents, neighbors or anyone.

Everyone had their critical opinions on my write ups, but that was now becoming a debatable topic, I concentrated on my work because I believed in it more than my critics.

My journals were on a great demand, as for Aarav, he still remained in touch with me as the same guy back in school who wanted to make me talk, just for the fun of it.

Dr. Agarwal was at the ashram as always, but never did a day go without talking to these two important life changing people.

Chapter 25

The milestone

It was not easy being a topic of discussion, but then again I felt a certain sense of responsibility towards people. They connected with my work, as the whole idea of our education system's inability to live up to a certain standard, was an open secret.

I was able to bring out that provocation into people to believe in what they wish to do. It made me believe in myself, I was now able to understand Dr. Agarwal's theory of how we heal by helping others.

I remained in contact with Dr. Agarwal and by now Aarav was a freelance Theatre artist, I was very sure from the beginning that he would take something "dramatic" like this as a career and he did it.

Years passed by, there were tons of reviews, comments, appreciations, interviews and book launch's everywhere. I was invited as a guest and it was the most interactive platform.

Until one morning when I received a call from the Publishing House in Bombay that was in search of a writer who is ready to go New Zealand for writing a biography of an old doctor.

At first I did not understand, why they picked New Zealand.

At first I wasn't prepared to do this as it was out of my comfort zone but it was a life-changing moment when it was a biography that they wished to develop on the life of their icon and inspiration, Dr. Agarwal!

How could I possibly say a no!

Though I did not know how this man was so influential in the life of other's. I was ready to do it. Dr. Agarwal is someone I was living my life that very moment. It was a life changing offer and I was ready to take up this major task. It was shocking to know that now Dr. Agarwal moved to New Zealand, which he never mentioned in most of our conversations.

This was a journey, which never ends.

Dr. Agarwal and Aarav's life were a mystery to me from the beginning. I was thrilled to start my work. The father and son were some of the rarest people whom I was curious to know about.

It was on this day that I moved out to New Zealand to begin one of my biggest books I was going to pendown.

At the airport, I had my parents, my best friends Seema and Shivani, my cousins Mahesh and Karan, my grandmother and most important of all my brother, whom I loved to bits – Vaibhav.

I stood there in front of them, who were all a part of my story hugging me tight with their endless love and support in the path I had chosen.

My mother was a completely changed person now, she was convinced that I was destined to become a writer and hugged me tight to give me strength and wish me good luck.

It was a warm, loving send off from the people I grew up with. This was a journey I was heading to on my own choice, I was again able to feel that happiness in my veins and in me when I first attended the prayer meet and read the slokah's in the ashram, it was the inner voice which was in sync with myself, without any more noises of any form. I was my complete self, I was looking forward for this journey, all my engineering friends had been left India but for education and job purpose, but this was something I was heading for out of the passion that has become my profession.

It never felt like a profession it was my life, I loved every minute of my day in writing, researching, interacting with my readers, searching for new ways to discuss many topics. My motive was more about bringing humanity, compassion and more understanding, through my journals among the fellow beings and celebrates even failure with the same zeal and not insult.

Chapter 26

University of Auckland

I sat there in my car thinking about all this and was ready with my notes for my speech for tomorrow.

It was 3 years ago that I had moved to New Zealand for my project, my most notable work in my career was going to release.

Life is so strange, all throughout I was this very unhappy person who felt so hard to live a normal existence, I clearly lived everybody's life but everything has it's expiry date.

I found the expiry date of steering me into the crowd's career choice's when I met Dr. Agarwal, the only way I can thank this man is by presenting his biography through my words. He made me realize my dream and I realized the energy I had built in me everytime I was swallowing the different hollow minded comments I was subjected to.

Today when I am here amidst my event managers, stage organizers, so many educated professors and the various intellectual guests in front of me. I feel a deep sense of gratitude towards the critics like Mrs. Lakshmi Gajapati Pillai, my relatives and everybody who got the chance to advice every time I couldn't fit into a crowd, who tried sabotaging my own identity, to Naina the girl who brought in me the essence of being an all rounder, Aarav who made me understand the value of happiness, my two best friends Seema and Shivani who stood by me and loved me like a sister.

My story seemed like a theatre play when I saw it as a third person, it made me see myself as a character which was so lost in these worldly comments which need not be given importance to if I had known what I was running after.

Realization of self-goals and the need to know the purpose of this existence is what made me understand that the world is filled with critics, but the craftsman is you and yourself. Only you can answer every step you take but these answers need not be justified to the entire neighborhood as long as you are aware of where you are heading to.

It was this little lesson that has brought me to this magnanimous University to deliver a speech today.

It was an inner call to shut those cynics' mouths who echoed their hollow opinions.

That was that one day I can never forget, that helped me shatter my fears, to let me become anything I wanted, as that is what they said!